I0691411

EXECUTIVE MESS

First Edition

Published by the Nazca Plains Corporation
Las Vegas, Nevada
2013

ISBN: 978-1-61098-299-3
E-Book: 978-1-61098-300-6

Published by
The Nazca Plains Corporation ®
4640 Paradise Rd, Suite 141
Las Vegas NV 89109-8000

PUBLISHER'S NOTE
Executive Mess is a work of fiction created wholly by *Christopher
Trevor's* imagination. All characters are fictional and any
resemblance to any persons living or deceased is purely by accident.
No portion of this book reflects any real person or events.

Cover Photo, DaniloAndjus
Art Director, Blake Stephens

DEDICATION

For Lady Shanna, thanks for the title…

EXECUTIVE MESS

First Edition

Christopher Trevor

CONTENTS

TAKEN FOR A RIDE
ON THE SUBWAY

It was rush hour on a hot, sticky day in August in New York City. Being dressed in a suit and tie with my white button down shirt sticking to my back and my nylon dress socked feet sweating in my leather wingtips, waiting for the uptown local train was not my idea of where I wanted to be at that moment. But fuck, I decided to make the best of it. While I was standing there on the crowded and hot platform was when I saw him. Typical construction worker outfit; mustard colored work boots, the tight, slightly too-short white tee shirt that didn't quite reach his pants, the well-worn blue jeans with a few holes that were clearly used for heavy-duty work. He was also belt-less, and although I generally prefer tight jeans on a guy, his were loose enough to have sagged down to expose just the top part of the crack of his ass, a not unpleasant vision I must say!

He stood about five-foot-ten and looked to weigh in at around 170 pounds or so, give or take, about two inches shorter and fifteen pounds lighter than me. He was nicely muscled and beefy, from working as a construction worker and perhaps working out at the gym as well? He had not yet gone to pot, as most construction workers seem to do by the time they reach thirty, *HAR, HAR, HAR*. He looked to be in his mid-20s or thereabouts, so I guessed that he had a few good years left in him. He had dark hair, curly enough to help make up for the fact that he was sporting a bad haircut.

He was drinking a beer from a can in a paper bag and he looked just slightly buzzed. I guessed that he had really worked hard and sweated in the sun that day working outdoors perhaps at his construction job site. I figured that if I played my cards right, I could follow him on board when the train came and see if that ass felt as good as it looked.

As the local train approached he finished his beer and tossed the can into the trash bin. Good boy, I thought, he's not a litter bug, *HAR, HAR, HAR*. I followed him onto the packed train like a shadow and let the crowd push my hand into the crack of his ass. It was nice and warm and we were scrunched together like sardines in a can. I said to myself, "No escape for this hunky guy!" As the train started to pull out of the station he started to turn. Let me tell you, this was no easy feat in a jam-packed subway car. I thought he was going to try to run away and ruin my fun as my hand lost its nesting place against his butt, and was left with nothing more than his side. I also thought he was going to face me head-on and say something like, "Yo bud, would you mind takin' your hand off my ass?" in construction worker accent and lingo. But instead he kept turning, and soon my hand was flush up against his fly. OMG, I could feel the buttons of his 501's, yet, better still, something was stirring behind them. Fuck, not only was he not running away, but he had obviously played this kind of game before. His ass crack being a tad on display was probably the lure he used.

He ground his crotch into my hand as I felt him stiffen. He seemed pretty big down there, though I couldn't tell for sure, so I decided that a different kind of fun was now in order. I slipped a finger between two buttons, and happily, it met with the cotton material of his underpants. I love the feeling of a studly guy's underpants against his hard cock. There's something so kinky about that thin cotton material against the hardness of a male's shaft. By the next stop I had all but the top and bottom buttons opened.

I maneuvered my crotch over to his hand, but he wasn't reciprocating. He did give me his crotch completely though, grabbing the metal support rod above his head with both hands and closed his sexy eyes. He locked his fingers together over the rod and sort of just hung there like a side of beef in a butcher's freezer, the muscles on his hairy arms flexing nicely and his tee shirt riding up further to expose a bit of his sexy midriff. I wondered if he was imagining himself strung up and helpless. I sure was!

I popped open the bottom button for better access to the seven plus inches of hard cock he was sporting in his underpants. I sidled my finger into the fly opening of his underpants and grabbed onto his thick, busy pubic hair and I could tell that he was the sort of guy who didn't do any trimming in that department. Damn, his dick was so hard I could take his pulse. I wondered how long it had been since this construction dude had shot a load. By now the train was at 18th Street, which meant only two more stops before the train would empty out at Penn Station, where most of the commuters get off. I could feel his pre cum seeping through the thin material of his underpants. He was dripping heavily now and I took advantage of the natural lube to give the head of his dick under his underpants a great going over. I could have easily pulled his cock out of his underpants and then out of his 501's, no one on the train had a clue what was happening here, but I would have much preferred to have him shoot his load in his underpants and wear his cum the rest of his trip home. Not to mention that besides a guy's underpants being real sexy on him there's something just so damned hot about filling those underpants with the guy's spunk. Besides, I didn't want him shooting off and messing up the subway car, the other passengers and myself. What a scene that would have been huh?

I increased the rhythm and intensity and a look of deeper satisfaction engulfed his ruggedly handsome face. That was all the acknowledgment I received. A look to himself and for himself! I don't even think he had looked to see who was doing him. I don't think he even cared if it was a man or woman working him over. I was still trying to figure out if I could make him blast off by the time we hit Penn Station, when the commuters would get off the train and the crowd would thin out, thus effectively ending our adventure.

The train pulled into the last stop before Penn Station and I realized he was completely oblivious to me. I was doing all the work and he was completely self-absorbed. Obviously there wasn't a whole lot in this for me.

That was when I decided to initiate plan B. I kept working his dick through his underpants, but as we pulled into Penn Station I pulled my hand out of his jeans and popped his top button, just as the subway doors opened. He still had both hands locked together on the support rod as his jeans hit the floor. I knew I would have to work fast for what I wanted to accomplish now. The crowd thinned out a bit almost instantly as people rushed off the train. I had stepped back by this point, ready to really work the construction dude over now. His pants' hitting the floor was like a wake-call interrupting a great dream for him it seemed. All of a sudden he must have realized that he was standing there with his jeans down around his work boots and socks, with a raging and pre cum oozing hard-on in his briefs, his white briefs, as I could now see them. He actually froze in place for a couple of seconds after he had opened his eyes.

"What the fuck?" he whispered as I clamped a hand around the hard-on in his briefs.

New York being New York, it seemed that not one of the commuters even noticed him in their rush to get off the train, although some of the passengers who stayed on and some who were getting on seemed to do a double-take as they first saw him, then proceeded to ignore him. It was still crowded enough that no one noticed the guy in the suit with his hand clamped around the construction dude's cock in his briefs. As for him, he was beet-faced as I gave his cock a hard pull and squeeze, setting him off in his briefs. I let go of him...

As he erupted in his briefs, grunting breathlessly, he struggled to quickly get his jeans up and to hide his spurting cock as it filled and filled his underpants. He was grunting and saying things like, "Holy fuck, *oooh* man, holy shit..."

His impressive dick was still dripping and spurting, filling his underpants as he shoved it into his jeans. I was happy to have had an unobstructed view of his rather fine ass as he was bending over to pull up his jeans. He had a construction worker tan... dark to the line of his pants or shorts, then pure white until just above the knees. It helped accent his ass very nicely, which was fairly hairless in contrast to his hairy legs. And bending over to hoist up his jeans with both hands, (still grunting as he spurted the last of his mess into his briefs) he actually gave me a nice quick glimpse of his rosebud, what I also sometimes refer to as a guy's pucker.

Once he had managed to put himself back together he just turned and stared at the doors which by this time had closed. He disembarked from the train at the next stop, his face still crimson red from embarrassment... and no doubt feeling all slimy in his underpants. I don't know if he realized that I was the one who had been fooling around with him, or if he thought he'd just had a real intense fantasy and that was why he had cum like gangbusters in his underpants. But his buttons popping open, he had to know that someone had done that to him. I wondered if he realized that I was still on the train. I have to say that this experience makes for a very *hot* memory.

SHORE LEAVE

by an anonymous cop
and Christopher Trevor

Story Inspired by: The Broadway Show and Movie "On the Town", 1960's Batman Episode "The Riddler's False Notion", and Alfred Hitchcock.

Todd took another long swig-and-swallow from his beer, leaned back in his chair and sighed contentedly.

"You know," he said. "This is just like that Frank Sinatra and Gene Kelly movie my girl back home made me watch one night before I shipped out. It was about three sailor boys on shore leave in New York City. They were seeing all the sights and really having a ball. Except, unlike the sailors in the movie we haven't picked up any girls yet."

Jason was looking over the bar they were in, a bar that their buddy Logan had dragged them to- in fact it was one of many bars that Logan had dragged them into. And as he looked over the place Jason figured that it was unlikely that they would pick up any pussy whatsoever in this place… because there weren't any females in sight. All Jason could see as he continued to look around were guys, guys and more guys, most of them in leather jackets and boots. He stifled a chuckle as he thought how he and his two sailor buddies really dressed the place up in their frosty white uniforms and black patent leather highly shined lace-up shoes. Jason thought to himself that this was probably one of those leather gay bars he had heard about… and as he thought some more he had to wonder why in all hell Logan had wanted to go there. Logan, Jason thought, is a great guy and a terrific shipmate… but still, the guy was a little strange. He always seemed to have something going on, something secret, and something strange. It was unusual that all the guys on the ship called him by his last name instead of his first, like everyone else. Hell, Jason wasn't even sure what Logan's first name was… Harry or Larry or Steve… yeah, that was it, Steve. But fuck, can't complain he went on thinking, Logan has shown us this city and man it's more than I ever imagined. And now this bar, and yes, it undoubtedly was a gay bar. Interesting place though, real tough looking men here, not the limp wrists one that Jason had always associated gay men with, but damn, be that as it may, what were they doing there? And where had Logan gone off to?

Then, a tall muscular guy in tight, tight jeans, leather boots that almost reached his knees, a tight black tee shirt that covered his chest and emphasized his well-built physique, and topped off with a leather vest, came over to the table where the sailors were seated.

"Can I buy you sailors a beer?" the man asked.

Jason wanted to say something, like tell the faggot to get lost, but Todd, sweet naïve Todd, replied first.

"Gee, thanks pal, but I think I've already had one too many," Todd said with a smile, glancing down at the several empty bottles on the table in front of him.

"How about you, Sailor boy?" the man asked, speaking directly to Jason, eyeing the older of the two sailors up and down.

"Thanks, but we have to head out," Jason said, not smiling. "It's almost past curfew. We're just waiting for our buddy. You uh, haven't seen him have you?"

"If you're referring to that other sailor boy in that sexy all white uniform, yeah, I saw him," the man said, sounding suggestive as hell. "He left through the back door with a couple of guys about twenty minutes ago. Out to buy some stuff I guess."

Oh shit, thought Jason. That damned Logan left them on their own again. Oh well, he thought, I better get young Todd here back to the hotel before he passes out. He did have one too many beers and this is definitely no place for a handsome young guy like him.

"Thanks pal," Jason said. Then to Todd he added, "Come on Sailor, we better head back while we can still make it. We can join up with Logan later."

The tall stranger stood there, eyeing the two young sailors.

"You don't have to rush off boys," the leather and booted man said. "There's still plenty of the night left and I'm sure we can have lots of fun if you stay around."

Jason pulled Todd up by one arm and steered him toward the exit.

"Thanks," he said. "But we're uh, not the type, sorry."

And with that the two sailors left the bar, headed out to the street and hailed the first cab that they saw.

Back at the two bit flea trap of a hotel that Logan had found for them on the West Side the two sailors headed to their room on the sixth floor. It was evident that Todd was dragging his ass; this city life was just too much for a country boy like him. When they entered the room Todd just dropped down onto one of the beds and in no time flat was snoring away. Jason simply sighed and once again felt a little envious of his younger shipmate. No point in trying to wake him to undress him or get him to take a piss or anything, he thought. He looked at the young handsome stud, muscles rippling from his early years working on the farm in Idaho or Wisconsin or whatever hick state he came from. Yes, Jason thought, the kid has a perfect body, which is great because it draws the women to us pretty quickly. But not at the bar they had been at that night. Jason slipped Todd's low quarter's shoes off the guy and marveled at the size of his friend's feet… size 12 doublewide, they were. Damn, they were big, so fucking big, beautifully formed digits and they looked perfect, so perfect in the tight fitting black nylon over the cuff regulation dress socks. Jason rubbed Todd's feet gently for a few seconds, feeling the muscles in the soles, then sighed and pulled one of the thin blankets over his buddy.

In fact Jason knew that his own body was pretty damn good too- well built, hard stomach and strong legs and arms. All this thanks to his Navy training. In fact, he sometimes thought that Logan took up with them because both sailors were magnets for pussy. And that puzzled Jason even more because if that were the case why had Logan hit so many of those bars in and around Greenwich Village? Could it be that Logan was queer? Nah, thought Jason, he'd seen Logan score with more than one available chick. No, it must be something else… but what?

The guy who had tried to buy them beers in the last club said that Logan had left with a couple of other guys and had gone to pick up something… or buy something? Drugs? Shit, Jason thought as he stripped down to his skivvies, I hope not. The last thing we need now is to get involved with drugs. Where the fuck was Logan and what was he up to this time? Jason sighed as he fell onto one of the other beds…

"I guess Logan will show up later and then we'll find out what it was all about," Jason said to himself as he laid his head on the pillow. "I wonder what that guy in the boots really wanted…"

Jason thought and thought more about the guy in the boots, what he had said about Logan, but like Todd he was soon sound asleep.

Jason wasn't sure how long he actually had been asleep… not long that was for sure… when the phone woke him up. Groggily, stumbling, he reached for the phone and located it on the dingy table between the beds. He wasn't much more awake when his hand finally found it and he lifted the receiver to his ear.

"Yea," Jason mumbled.

The voice on the other end, raspy and sounding like it was in pain, screamed out, "Jason, Jason… help me. Help me please." This woke the young sailor up totally with a start.

"Logan, Logan, is that you?" Jason asked, his voice trembling as he gripped the receiver. "What the fuck is happening… where are you man?"

"Help me Jason… they're coming… oh shit… help," the voice on the other end of the phone pleaded.

"Where are you Logan?" Jason asked. "What do you need?"

"Outside… I'm outside… I'm blindfolded man…" Logan responded. "I'm, okay, now I'm not blindfolded and I'm… *no, no… please… oh shit… shit… Jason!*"

And with that the phone went dead.

Shit, thought Jason. *What the fuck?*

He jumped out of bed and began to throw on his uniform, pulling the white trousers up over his legs at the same time yelling at his roommate Todd who had snored contentedly throughout the entire episode.

"Todd, *Todd*, wake up man," Jason thundered. "Logan is in trouble. We have to help him."

The young sailor came awake almost immediately and once again it amazed Jason that he could snap out of a sound sleep so quickly. Jason had seen Todd do this before – crawl out of the bunk after being deep in dreams and in seconds be ready for duty. Part of living on the farm, he guessed. Quickly, as the two sailors put on their shoes the older sailor explained to the younger one what had just occurred.

"I don't know anything more except that Logan sounded like he was being murdered or something," Jason prattled. "He said he was blindfolded, and then he said he wasn't blindfolded… and then he screamed my name. He said he was outside. We gotta check it out."

The two sailors finished dressing and rushed out of their room. Jason decided that they could make better time on the stairs than wait for the rickety elevator and the two literally flew down the stairs two or three at a time. Todd made it out the front door first and was a little startled to note that it was still dark. He automatically checked his watch and saw that it was only 4:05 AM. Jason came right up behind Todd and then the two stood there on the deserted sidewalk wondering what to do next.

That's when they heard the screams; Logan's unmistakable deep voice coming to them from above. The two sailors looked questioningly at each other… and then they looked upwards at the roof of the ten-story hotel building… and there they spotted a sight that made them both gasp. There was their buddy Logan, his arms seemingly pinned behind him… tied? Cuffed? Jason quickly wondered… balanced… but teetering dangerously on the ledge of the hotel building… the ledge that was just below the roof.

"*Oh God, help me!*" Logan screamed miserably, looking down at his two buddies on the street below.

"Oh my God," Todd said. "It's Logan. He's gonna fall… he'll be killed."

Logan's white uniform was clearly visible from the ground as he stood there perilously balanced on the ledge of the hotel building. Jason had to wonder how their sailor buddy had wound up in such a fucked up predicament. He recalled Logan on the phone saying he was outside… that he was blindfolded… and then he said he wasn't blindfolded. It came together in a sick fashion in Jason's mind. Somehow someone had captured Logan, tied him, blindfolded him and then led him out onto the ledge where he now stood. Then, something came hurling down from the ledge and landed next to the two dumbstruck sailors. They looked down and saw that it was a shoe; immediately recognizable as a regulation U. S. Navy patent leather issue. Then, another shoe came down and the two men knew that they were Logan's shoes and that their buddy was trapped, tied and standing on his socked feet up on that ledge. The shoes, being that they were navy issued also told the two sailors that someone indeed had captured their buddy and set him in the horrendous position he was now in.

"Damn, he won't be able to maintain his balance up there," Jason said. "We'll have to get up there and somehow get him down."

Jason grabbed Logan's shoes and together he and Todd rushed back into the building- no one was at the front desk to see or stop them… and damn, there was no phone in sight with which they could have called the police with. Both sailors had left their cell phones in their room. Todd, in better shape, in the lead and Jason thinking to himself that all the PT that they had to undertake in training was at this moment paying off. He had no idea how long it actually took them to reach the top floor, figure out where the door to the roof was and to burst through it. The two sailors dashed out onto the roof and over to the edge where they had spotted their buddy on the ledge just below the roof... but he wasn't in sight.

"Damn," thought Jason as he panted. "He fell..."

But as he and Todd looked over the edge of the roof they could tell that there was no body on the ground below. They stood there, baffled. Where the fuck had Logan gone? What in all hell was happening?

"Jason," Todd said, sounding winded. "I don't understand. Where's Logan? What's going on?"

"I don't know buddy, I don't know," Jason replied. "Someone put Logan out there on that ledge... and they probably took him with them while we were running up the stairs and..."

Suddenly, the door to the roof opened and two men came out onto the roof. One was nothing less than a giant... close to seven feet tall and bulging with solid muscle. And he looked mean... no, not just mean Jason thought, he looked terrifying. The other man was of average size, about five feet nine or ten, dressed in chinos and a brown leather jacket. Where the giant had looked mean, this guy looked like pure evil.

"Boys," said the average sized guy. "I assume you're looking for your pal Logan."

Jason was the one to answer.

"What the fuck is going on here?" Jason asked. "Where is Logan? He was standing on that ledge... We have his shoes here..."

Jason held up his buddies' shoes...

"Boys, boys, calm down," the average sized man said with a grin. "Your buddy is fine... for the moment. We're holding him in a safe place and if you do what we tell you he'll be set free and the three of you can return to your boat or whatever it is you sailed here on and be on your merry way. And once you're on your way you'll have exciting tales to tell your buddies about… all about your adventures in the Big Apple."

"Logan was on the ledge of this building…" Todd began.

"And now he's not…" the average sized man said.

"Who the fuck are you and what do you want?" Jason asked. "Where is Logan?"

"Boys, I'm sure you both know what it is we want," the man said. "Your boat's last port of call was Beirut in Lebanon. Logan picked up a package there and he was supposed to deliver it here to us. He doesn't have it boys; he claims he lost it. To our way of thinking that's not likely. You see, we want that package boys, and if we don't get it – and get it soon – your boy Logan will no longer sail the seven seas… rather he'll fly off the ledge… the next time we balance him on one…"

Todd, moving toward the two men in a menacing manner, shouted, "It's a ship, not a boat, and don't call us boys!" Jason stepped forward and pulled his buddy back because he noticed the giant pull what was obviously a gun from his pocket. No way was Jason going to let the young sailor get shot.

"Boat, ship, canoe… makes no difference to us," the man said with a shrug. "But we want that package. We figure that if Logan doesn't have it… and we have proof that he had it when you started this vacation of yours… that means one of you must have it. So, turn it over to us and we will let you all go on your way with no one getting hurt."

Jason spoke up now.

"We don't know anything about any package," Jason said, almost pleading. "What is it supposed to be… drugs?"

"No, not something as common as drugs," the man replied and playfully and brazenly tugged on Jason's neckerchief. "It's something far more valuable. Now, where is it?"

As the man spoke he lustfully tugged on and handled Jason's neckerchief, the sailor didn't dare pull away or push the man's hand away.

"I don't know anything about any package or where it is," Jason seethed and then the man let go of his neckerchief. "If Logan had it then he still has it."

"No, we checked," the man replied. "He doesn't have it any more. We've kept pretty good tabs on you sailor boys since you arrived here and it doesn't look as if Logan passed it on to anyone. So therefore, you boys either have it or you know where it is. And we want it."

Todd, obviously fighting mad, said, "Fuck you and your package. Tell us where Logan is now. We have to be back on board by twenty three hundred hours or we will be AWOL."

The man looked at the two sailors and Jason was taken aback by the pure malice in his grin and the evil dripping from his voice when he said, "Well then, that gives you plenty of time to find the package and return it to us. So, stop wasting time boys. We'll see you back here on the roof at nine tonight… don't know what that would be in your navy talk. You have the package… we have Logan… you give us the package… we'll give you Logan… you don't… well… think about it. Your sailor buddy didn't look all that happy balanced on that ledge down there did he? And if I were you boys I wouldn't contact the authorities. It won't go well for your friend if we find out that you did."

With that, the giant, silent up until this point laughed and pulled a big ugly looking GLOCK from his belt, pointed it at the two sailors and told them to get on their stomachs and to count slowly to a hundred before getting up. Jason and Todd knew that they had no choice in the matter. They lay down flat on the rooftop. They heard, more than witnessed, the two men leave through the roof door and then they waited several more minutes before getting up.

"Gee Jason, what are we gonna do?" Todd asked, sounding miserable.

"I don't know Todd," Jason responded. "Maybe we should contact the Shore Patrol or even the New York City police… but damn, you heard what he said. We do that and Logan's a dead man. Let's go back down to our room and think this over carefully."

The two sailors climbed back down the stairs to the sixth floor and to their room. When they entered they were shocked to see that someone else had been there since they left and had given their belongings a complete shakedown. Clothes were tossed everywhere; their duffle bags were turned inside out. Dresser drawers were pulled out and strewn on the floor. To put it plainly the place was a mess.

"Shit," said Todd. "I bet they were here looking for that damned package. What do you think it is Jason and where is it?"

Picking up his stuff and putting it in order, Jason responded, "I don't know the answer to either question buddy. Did you ever see Logan with any kind of package?"

"No, but he was pretty damned secretive about things," Todd replied. "I accidentally opened his drawer in the bureau there and he went ape. He yelled at me, which was totally unlike him."

"Hmm, I'd guess that's where he kept his mysterious package, whatever the hell it is," Jason said. "What we have to do is go over everything we did since coming here and see if we can spot something unusual on Logan's part. Do you remember where we went the first day?"

"Well, we took a cab from the ship to this hotel," Todd replied. "I remember Logan specifically saying this hotel because he said it was something we could afford. He knew about it. After we checked in and unpacked we all went out and had a big breakfast. I also recall two of the waitresses at the diner we went to really checking us out and…"

And so it went, the two sailors mentally retracing their steps since arriving in New York, trying to find some clue as to what Logan was up to and what might have happened to that mysterious package.

Meanwhile, in a private room in the hotel's basement, a naked Logan lay spread eagle on a dirty bed, his hands and feet firmly tied to the bedposts. The two men from the roof and two others surrounded the bed. The evil looking one, mentioned by the others only by the name "Boss" was talking to the trembling, terrified and naked sailor.

"Now this has gone far enough asshole," the man said to Logan. "Tell us where the package is or else… we'll put you back out on that ledge and this time we'll leave you there till you lose your balance and plunge ten stories to your bloody demise."

"I–I don't know, honest," Logan muttered. "I had it at the bottom of my duffle bag, safe, but when I went to get it tonight it was gone. I swear to you, I don't know what happened."

"You think one of your two buddies took it?" the man asked and as he asked this question the Boss accidentally brushed his fingers against the bare sole of Logan's foot, creating an instant twitch and groan from the captive sailor.

"Well, well," said the Boss. "It looks as if our sailor boy here is ticklish."

And with that the Boss began to lightly trail his fingers across the bound sailor's feet, causing Logan to jump and squirm and laugh and moan.

"No, please," Logan cried. "Don't do that!"

The Boss motioned to the other two men and they sensed immediately what he wanted. They eagerly approached the sailor, waiting for their chance to administer tickle tortures.

"Just tell us where the package is and we'll stop," the Boss intoned. "Did those two yokel friends of yours take it?"

"I don't know, honest... I don't..." Jason began, but he never got further because the two men began in earnest to tickle him, their fingers magically playing with his bare feet.

The sailor thrashed on the bed, laughing hysterically, moaning, groaning, begging them to stop in between breaths. But the men were apparently expert at this type of torture and soon had added other areas of Logan's body to their talented fingers. They worked his armpits, his belly, even behind and around his ears... and finally his balls and crotch. The sailor screamed and laughed louder, pleading with them to stop, pulling at his bonds in a futile attempt to escape. Periodically they would stop for a few moments and the Boss would ask again about the package, but Logan held firm in his denials of not knowing what had happened to it. Sweat was pouring off the captive sailor as the men played gently and evilly on his body. Finally, Logan could take it no more and passed out.

"What do you think Boss?" one of the men asked. "Is he telling the truth?"

"It appears so," the Boss replied. "I can't imagine anyone withstanding tickling that bad, but still, it makes no sense. What in the hell could have happened to that damned package? DAMN! Get some water and revive this asshole... and then continue tickling him until he confesses. Monk and I have got to go make some phone calls. We'll be back in a couple of hours. If he tells you anything new call me on my cell phone and let me know."

"What about the other two sailors, Boss?" the man asked. "Should we watch them?"

"Good question, but no, I don't think so," the Boss replied. "They both look too stupid to have taken the package, but they might have a clue as to what our boy Logan here did with it. I think we'll just leave them alone and let them find it for us. If we don't get that package back soon, we're all in trouble."

And with that he and the giant left.

The two men looked at their captive sailor boy, one of them licking his lips in anticipation of the fun they were going to have with the muscular serviceman.

"Okay then, let's get to work on Popeye here," he said with a grin and grabbed Logan's cock.

Not knowing what else to do Todd and Jason decided that they should get some coffee and food in them to keep up their energy. They went to an all-night coffee shop on the corner where they had had breakfast the first morning that they had been in New York City. They took a booth by the window and as the waitress ogled them they ordered breakfast.

Todd, in between bights into his pancakes and eggs said, "What are we gonna do Jason?" We can't let them kill Logan."

"I know, but damn Todd we aren't equipped to solve this," Jason responded. "I really think we should go back to the ship and tell the captain and Lieutenant Trevor. They'll know what to do. We'll just have to take our chances on Logan getting through this. Shit, for all we know he's already dead."

Just then Jason spotted the Boss and Monk exiting the alley to the rear of the hotel.

"Look," Jason said to his buddy. "There are those two ass wipes. Listen, here's what we'll do. I'll follow them; maybe they'll lead me to Logan. While I do that you go back to the ship and get help. We'll meet back at the hotel as soon as we can. Hopefully when we get back to the hotel I'll have Logan with me."

"But Jason…" the young sailor started to say.

"Quick, hurry, they're heading down that other street," Jason said. "I'll tail them. Now, go!"

With that Jason was out of the booth and out on the street. Todd sighed, took another bight of his breakfast, left some money on the table and headed out to catch a taxi that would take him to his ship. What he had wanted to tell Jason before he ran off half-cocked was that they had again left their cell phones in the hotel room...

Jason quickly caught up with the two men and began following them at a discrete distance. They didn't seem to be in any hurry so Jason didn't have much trouble keeping up. And as it was becoming later in the morning more of the working people of New York City were out and about. Suited men and women were everywhere all of a sudden. The boss had a cell phone and was talking on it as he and the other man walked. Jason wished he could hear what was being said but he couldn't risk getting any closer. Then, the two men turned a corner and when Jason rounded it he was surprised to see that the two men were nowhere in sight. The sailor was slightly baffled but then noticed a door on a building on the other side of the street closing. He argued with himself for a moment, wondering what to do and then said to himself, "Fuck it, I've got to see if that's where they went." He hurried across the street and stepped cautiously to the door, opening it slowly and stepping inside a dark hallway. It smelled dank and musty. He heard voices at the far end of the corridor coming from behind a closed door and he crept closer to see if he could hear what was being said. When Jason reached the spot he put his ear next to the door and heard the boss saying, "We have the sailor but the package is missing. We're trying to get him to talk but it seems he has no idea what happened to the package. He has a couple of buddies who..." And that was the last thing Jason remembered as the giant had silently snuck up behind him in the hall and with one blow knocked him unconscious.

Todd made it back to the ship and immediately went to the captain to explain what had happened. The captain called in Lieutenant Trevor, the ship's security officer and the two questioned Todd thoroughly, initially finding it difficult to believe his story. But it was obvious that the young sailor was panicking and telling the truth. Todd swore to his superior officers that he had no idea what the package was or what had happened to it. And he also swore that he didn't know what Logan had been up to or why he was "smuggling" (that was the word they decided on) something.

After consultation on what to do, the decision was that the Lieutenant, along with a group of Shore Patrol men would go with Todd back to the hotel and investigate. When they arrived Todd took them to his room but nothing had changed there. The SP's checked the room carefully, looking for the mysterious package, but found nothing. They then went up on the roof to check it out but again no real clues were discovered.

They went to the lobby and at this hour there was a desk clerk on duty. He was an older man in his sixties, slightly deaf and anything but cooperative. He simply had no idea what the dumb ass sailor boy was talking about.

"Evil mystery men, missing packages, bullshit," the desk clerk scoffed, looking at Todd with anger in his eyes. "I think this young man probably had too much to drink last night."

That was all the desk clerk had to offer in the way of help.

Lieutenant Trevor decided that they should check out the hotel and broke the group up, starting with the top floor, instructing them to look for anything unusual. Todd joined the group heading to the basement of the hotel.

The basement area was pretty much a mess with trash and boxes lying all around. Todd spotted a closed door at one end of the area and headed toward it. He pushed open the door and was shocked to see two men leaning over a bed where a naked man was tied. The men were startled to see Todd in his sailor uniform and they rushed at him, but Todd was in great shape and well trained. He was able to knock one of them to the floor. However, the other man was quick and soon had Todd tackled. By then the two SP's who had been with Todd rushed in and in short time the men were overtaken and cuffed.

Todd looked at the unconscious body on the bed and knew immediately that it was his buddy Logan.

"Oh my God, Logan, what happened?" Todd asked, but his buddy was badly beaten, his face was all bloodied and his chest was purple and black with bruises. He could not speak. Lieutenant Trevor came rushing in with the rest of the SP's, recognized immediately what had happened and radioed for an ambulance. After the EMT personnel had come and taken Logan away to a hospital the lieutenant turned to Todd and said, "Okay, we have your friend Logan, but where is your other shipmate?"

"I don't know," the worried sailor said. "He was following the other two men the last I saw him."

"Well, we'll interrogate those two thugs and see if they can tell us anything," the lieutenant said. "Meanwhile I think we should all head back to the ship."

As Jason gradually came to consciousness he became aware that his wrists were tightly tied behind his back. His focus started to return and he saw that he was in a dark room, obviously a cellar type of room, with no windows. Since he wasn't tied to the chair he was sitting in he tried to stand up, tried to undo the ropes binding his hands. But then he heard a deep, foreign sounding voice behind him say, "Well, my little sailor boy is awake. Sit back down in the chair boy… or I'll make you."

Jason whirled around and spotted Monk the giant standing there, a grin on his face and a sparkle in his dark eyes.

"What the fuck?" the sailor said, but before he could say anything more Monk punched him in the stomach. "*HOOOFFF...*"

Jason collapsed on the floor.

Using just one arm the giant lifted the muscular sailor and set him down forcibly on the chair.

"You do what the fuck I tell you to do Sailor boy, or else," Monk said. "Got that?"

"Fuck you asshole," was Jason's sputtered response.

"Ah good, the sailor boy has some spunk in him," Monk laughed. "So much better. It's no fun when they give in too easily. I like working a boy like you until you promise me anything to stop."

Jason was taken aback by this and admitted to himself that this giant could tear him apart without much effort. The sailor simply stared back at him. It was then that the door opened and the boss entered.

"He awake yet Monk?" the boss asked.

"Yes Sir, just now Boss," Monk replied.

The boss faced the seated and tied Jason and looked him straight in the eyes.

"Okay Sailor boy, here's the story," the boss began. "You answer my questions, we let you go. Understand?"

But Jason just glared at him until the giant stepped forward with a menacing look, then he nodded his head.

"Good, now first of all, why were you following us?" the boss asked.

"To see if you'd lead me to where you're keeping Logan," Jason replied.

"Ah Logan, that fuck," the boss said. "Don't worry, he's in good hands. Now tell me what you know about my package."

"I told you, I don't know shit about any package," Jason seethed. "The first I heard about it was when you mentioned it on the roof of the hotel."

"Logan didn't tell you about it?" the boss asked and Jason shook his head no. "So in that case what are you and your other sailor buddy doing to find it for me?"

"I spotted you leaving the hotel and decided to follow you," Jason said. "I didn't know what else to do. My buddy Todd has gone back to the ship to notify our captain."

At that the boss swung his leather-covered hand back and rapped the sailor hard across his face.

"*HOOOFFF...*" Jason sputtered.

"You stupid asshole," the boss reeled. "I warned you about alerting the authorities. *Fuck,* now everything is screwed up. Monk, I've got to report this. Take care of this fuck head and then meet me at the usual place."

Monk the giant looked at the boss, then at Jason and said, "Gee boss, he's kind of cute. Can I first just... well, you know?"

Jason looked up at the giant and the boss in shocked revulsion.

"Do whatever you want," the boss replied miserably. "Just make sure to meet me in four hours."

With that the boss left the room.

Monk stood in front of the now very nervous Jason, looking down at him and grinning dumbly.

"You heard the boss Sailor boy, you're mine now," the giant said. "Mine to play with and enjoy."

"What the fuck are you gonna do?" Jason asked.

"Ah my handsome sailor boy, I'm going to use you," Monk replied. "I'm going to use you and satisfy myself with you. Like the boss said, I'm going to do whatever I want and if you don't cause me any problems I just might let you go, *ha, ha!*"

Jason clenched his teeth, stood up and tried to head butt the giant in the stomach, but it seemed more like he was butting his head against a stone wall.

"Ah my little man, I can't have you jumping up and down and trying to fight me," Monk laughed. "Let's see… ah yes, here's some rope. I'll just have to tie you down."

With that he picked Jason up with one hand and tied the rope around the already bound wrists of the sailor. He then looped the other end of the rope over some pipes on the ceiling and yanked the struggling sailor up taut so that his muscular arms were bent upwards and his feet were just about touching the floor. Monk walked in front of Jason and with that the sailor tried kicking him.

"*Ah*, still some fight in you I see, good," Monk chuckled. "But I can't have you kicking at me while I…"

With that, Monk took more rope and tied Jason's ankles spread eagle to radiators on each side of the room. The sailor was now stretched out and totally helpless. He watched miserably as Monk went to a gym bag that was on the floor and pulled out a large, very sharp looking hunting knife. He stepped over to Jason, put the blade of the knife under Jason's chin and said, "You'd better behave Sailor boy or I'm gonna see your blood all over this nice floor." Jason's eyes opened as wide as saucers and he tried to back away, but of course being tied the way he was, it was impossible for him to move.

Monk ran the knife playfully over Jason's body… his neck, face, chest and horror of horrors, even his crotch. The sailor tensed up but did not say anything. Then, without warning the giant began to cut away Jason's uniform, slicing it in pieces. In very short order the handsome sailor was stripped to his skivvies, his socks and shoes.

"Now that's better," Monk giggled fiendishly. "Now I can see what I have here. Hmm… nice body, sailor boy. Yes, very nice indeed. I am going to enjoy it."

"You perverted sadistic asshole, *let me go!*" Jason cried out.

But of course the giant had no intention whatsoever of doing that. A couple more slices of the knife and Jason was totally naked from his ankles up. Monk put the knife down on a table and began to fondle the sailor's balls and cock.

"*MMMMM…*" the giant sighed. "Nice… real nice…"

Then, he hugged Jason's body close to his and began nibbling on the sailor's nips, making him cry out some more. At the same time the giant's hands laced behind Jason's back and soon his fingers began penetrating and exploring the sailor's shit-hole.

"NO, no… stop…" Jason pleaded.

But there was no stopping the giant. Jason could feel Monk's cock begin to grow and stiffen as it lay against his own crotch. He watched as Monk reached down and began to slowly stroke it.

"SHIT NO… don't do this to me man," the sailor reeled out in anticipation of what Monk was planning.

But Monk paid no attention as he stepped behind Jason and began massaging and kneading the sailor's ass cheeks.

"Beautiful," was all he said as he prepared himself to penetrate the gaping hole.

Just at that moment the door burst open and a tall muscular figure came into the room.

"Ah Monk, I see that you're up to your old tricks," the intruder said mockingly. "The only way you can get a piece of ass is to kidnap it and tie it up. Don't worry Sailor boy, his cock isn't big enough to cause you any damage."

With that Monk let go of Jason and roared at the intruder, "You son of a bitch, what are you doing here?"

"Looking for you Monk, bay, I need my own cock sucked," was the reply.

Jason watched in horrified fascination as Monk lunged at the intruder. In Jason's opinion there was no contest; Monk was the bigger of the two in height and weight. But the stranger was far more agile than the lumbering giant, and as Monk lunged at him, he stepped aside. As Monk then slipped by the man hit him over the head with a heavy piece of metal pipe. Jason has no idea where the pipe had come from but he assumed the man had had it in his hand all along. The blow stunned the giant and slowed him down, but it didn't stop him. When he turned back to the man however, he was hit again, this time square in the face, right on the nose, and blood spurted out. Monk was confused and that was all the stranger needed. Three or four more solid blows and Monk collapsed unconscious on the floor. The man took a pair of handcuffs from the back of his belt and cuffed the giant's wrists behind his back. Then, he stepped over to Jason and untied the sailor's ankles. He used the strands of ropes that he had taken off Jason's ankles to tightly tie the giant's feet together and then pulled his legs up and tied them to his wrists in a perfect hogtie position.

So much had happened so fast that Jason really hadn't looked carefully at the stranger who had rescued him. However, when the man came over closer to finish untying the hurting sailor, Jason saw his face.

"I know you," Jason said. "You were at that sleazy bar the other night. You wanted to buy us a drink. What the fuck is going on here?"

The man leaned close to him and Jason could smell the faint but somehow arousing aroma of leather and sweat on him. The man untied the rope holding Jason to the ceiling pipes and then caught the sailor as he dropped, his body not yet ready to stand on its own. Jason felt a little charge of excited electricity pass through him as the man held him in his arms. It felt good and at the same time it confused the sailor… was he attracted to this stranger?

"Yes, that was me, Sailor," the man said. "You should have stayed in the club and took me up on my offer. You would have been safer. I was only trying to help you. I had seen Logan get himself forced to join the Boss and Monk here and I felt that you guys would have been next. I was watching Logan but there was nothing I could do once they took him."

"But who the fuck are you… and what the fuck is going on?" Jason asked.

The man used Monk's knife to cut the final ropes from Jason's wrists and then took them in his own strong hands. He rubbed the circulation back into the sailor's wrists.

"My name is unimportant and let's just say that I work with Navy Intelligence," the man said. "Logan was working with us in our attempts to stop these guys from obtaining valuable intelligence info of strategic importance."

Jason, still in the arms of the man who had saved him, said, "The package… what was in the package?"

"A couple of microchips with some highly classified intelligence on them," the man replied. "If those chips fell into the wrong hands then there would have been a lot of trouble. But we managed to get into your hotel room and confiscate them before the Boss and Monk here could get to them. Logan was supposed to meet them at the leather bar and that's when I and my men were set to arrest them. But things got out of hand. So we had to change plans, but by then they had taken your friend Logan."

The man released his hold on Jason and asked him if he felt strong enough to stand on his own. Jason just nodded but to himself he thought, 'Damn, having this guy hold me like that was somehow exciting.'

"Well Sailor boy… although I probably should say Sailor man because you are indeed a man… I've got to head out now," the man said. "I'll notify your Lieutenant Trevor, who is pretty much aware of what has been going on, and he'll come here to get you. You keep an eye on Monk there and if he comes to, just hit him again. I'll also tell your lieutenant to bring you a new uniform as you can't return to your ship naked like you are."

"Logan… and Todd… what happened?" Jason asked.

"I'm afraid Logan got beat up pretty bad and he's in the hospital now," the man replied. "But he should recover okay. As for your young buddy, he's fine, maybe a little confused over all this, but then again, I would suppose you all are. Anyhow, as I said, I've got to run. We still have to corner the Boss and hopefully find out the powers behind all of this."

The man prepared to leave and at the door he turned back to Jason and said, "Yeah, it's too bad you left the club so early that night. I'm sure we really could have had some fun." Jason stammered, "Will… will I ever see you again?" But the man had left and the sailor did not know if he had heard. Jason looked down at the still unconscious Monk, gave him a hard kick in the ribs and sat down to wait for his lieutenant to come get him. All Jason could think was, yeah, this was some shore leave.

Six months later Logan, Jason and Todd, in their best dress uniforms, stood at attention in a small auditorium in the Pentagon. They were being awarded medals for what they had done. A high-ranking naval official was reading the citation, citing how through the heroic efforts of the three men, a dangerous enemy cell had been smashed. Todd beamed in boyish delight, Logan smiled happily, but Jason, well, Jason could only look at the handsome civilian in the suit and tie who stood on the other side of the room. The sailor thought to himself, "Yes, even out of the boots and leather and in a suit that is one handsome and exciting man." And Jason felt his heart jump a little when the man looked directly at him and winked.

THE CLIENT

by Alan Skram

Where do I start? Let's begin with me telling you that I'm in the supply business. I run a specialty business for a very selective, very discerning, wealthy clientele. If the client and the money are right I procure certain items for them. Maybe it would be better if I gave you an example. Let's say that you are a successful, wealthy, and powerful man, but you have a taste for a little something considered to be very taboo… and every once in a while you would like to sex up a hot guy, just to satisfy something that your loving wife cannot. If you are one of these select few that know how to get in touch with me then you can call and place an order… providing me with the specifics about what you are looking for.

If you personally know the item you wish to purchase you can provide locale and description. If you wish my company to procure someone matching the details provided and let's just say for this document the following description- between 25 and 30 years of age, in great physical shape, with black hair, approximately six feet tall, a beautiful smile and right now you'd prefer someone in law enforcement. Let's say you are visiting Chicago on business next month and would like for me to arrange a meeting with this particular person… and for the right price I can make it happen.

In Chicago I would call my associates and have them begin a search in the city and surrounding areas for a policeman that fits my client's specific tastes. If a guy meeting this criterion cannot be found locally, well, then I contact another associate and one can be obtained elsewhere and shipped privately to the specified location. For the sake of this telling a person of said description had been located.

His name was Officer Reynolds. He was 28 years old. He had been on the police force for only two years. He had never married but had been dating the same woman for the last seven months. He had done very well in the academy, he was extremely attractive with black hair, blue eyes and he even had dimples. He fit my client's list perfectly. I had also obtained a young handsome fireman as a back up. I believe in always giving the clients options. Officer Reynolds was so handsome that I almost kept him for myself. Who knows, I still might have a little fun with the cop after my client is finished with him.

I had my employees begin following Officer Reynolds to document his lifestyle. When my team researches a person I end up knowing more about them than they sometimes do about themselves. To make this part of my job easier I am glad to say that humans are so predictable and they usually follow the same daily routine. One important thing to know are their days off from work. If you obtain someone on their days off less suspicions are raised by their family and friends… and once returned to their lives they can most of the time account for having been missing for one or two days. Another aspect that has allowed me to operate for years undetected is that men will usually not report to the authorities that what they had been made to do during their days off due to total and utter embarrassment.

My client was coming to town on a Sunday and staying through the week.

This worked well because Officer Reynolds' nights off were Monday and Tuesday. I guessed that he hadn't been on the force long enough to be able to get good days off. I was to procure the handsome officer right after his shift finished on Sunday. That way he would be dressed in uniform, as requested by my client. As soon as he left work he would get in his car and drive to the drycleaners and pick up his extra uniforms, then he would stop at one of the fast food restaurants he usually frequents to pick up some food for his dinner which he would store in his refrigerator, go home and change, go to the gym and then over to his girlfriend's house. Well, that's what the cop would normally do on his day off, but not this time.

Like clockwork he got off work, said good-bye to his fellow officers, got in his car and drove directly to the drycleaners. As he then pulled into the fast food restaurant parking lot one of my employees drove past his car fast, very fast actually, almost sideswiping his. My employee parked and right on cue his actions had made Officer Reynolds angry.

The cop approached my employee shouting out, "Where the hell did you learn to drive?" and "I'm a cop, I'm off duty, but you're getting a ticket anyway bud!" blah, blah, blah, the usual cop jargon and after a few minutes my employee was saying that he was sorry. They both returned to their cars, my employee to his "borrowed" vehicle, and just in case you missed it "borrowed" means stolen. Just before re-entering his vehicle my employee decided to approach Officer Reynolds to apologize once more. As my employee began talking to the cop, going on about how he has the utmost respect for police officers, Officer Reynolds rolled down the window just in time to feel a Taser gun press into his shoulder. While the cop was stunned my employee simply moved him across the seat and got into his driver's seat while another of my hires came out of the restaurant and got into the car as well, in the backseat, and they drove off with the now captive officer in hand…

After having subdued Officer Reynolds and handcuffing him with his own cuffs, my employee placed a chloroform soaked rag over the cop's nose and mouth. Then, he pulled a cloth bag over Officer Reynolds' head and drove to an obscure location where the cop was then transferred into one of our vans and taken to an undisclosed location.

Thus, Officer Reynolds awoke to find himself still handcuffed and his ankles tied tightly together. His eyes blinked, trying to adjust to his surroundings, which was no more than a 20x20 Plexiglas cube. He was lying on the makeshift bed in the middle of the cube and instantly began to struggle and squirm, straining against his handcuffs and bonds. He shouted out into the cube, "Where the fuck am I?", "What the hell do you want with me?", and he heard nothing in return. Watching him squirm in his bondage I will admit again that it crossed my mind more than once to keep this hot, helpless cop all to myself. Hell, I still might have a little fun with him anyway.

In my profession you cannot simply leave the client in a confined space with an angry, bound, straight captured man without training that abducted guy first. I entered the warehouse, unlocking the door to the cube containing the hot hunky cop. Laying on his side his head whipped around to see who was coming in, his eyes open wide in fear and total confusion.

"What do you want with me?" he asked.

I sat on the side of the bed, reached down and placed my hand on his hip, giving it a gentle squeeze. I told him that a very important admirer of his wished to meet him and to also spend a little time getting to know him better. Of course when he heard that it only caused him to struggle and squirm more. He threw meaningless threats at me like, "You're going to jail, kidnapping a cop is a federal offense," and of course the one I always hear, "You better let me go now or else!"

After he was done ranting I said, "Now, let me lay down the ground rules for you Officer, One, I have a man who is going to use your muscular well-toned body for sex. Two, you will do whatever he tells you to do. Three, if you do as you're told you will be let go. However, if you do not do as you're told number three no longer applies. Now, do you understand everything I've told you?"

From his position on the floor where he was laying he simply looked up at me in shock. I took that look to mean "Yes," so I said, "Let's try a little test cop," and I reached down again and this time between his legs and grabbed the good-sized bulge that he was sporting. This made the cop push his hips away from me and kick out at me with his bound legs.

"Like hell I'm going to just lay there and let some faggot touch me?" the cop seethed.

What he didn't know was that was exactly what my client wanted, so just for fun I jumped down and landed on top of the bound up cop, pinning his body with mine. I reached around and really grabbed his cock this time. Feeling his hot, round ass pushing up against me was, shall we say, I considered it a perk.

My client was picked up from his hotel room, blindfolded and brought to the warehouse. With the help of my assistants Officer Reynolds was still bound in his uniform, arms behind his back and secured at the waist now with shackles on his muscular legs. He was placed next to the wall with a collar around his neck and secured to eyelet rings in the ceiling. His shackled legs were spread and tied off to hooks on each wall. The cube he was in was flooded with light and the surrounding area was completely dark. Upon entering the warehouse the client's blindfold was removed.

"Hello Sir, how was your trip?" I asked my wealthy client.

"Fine, just fine," he replied. "And I've been looking forward to this all day. It's all I was thinking about during my business meetings."

"Well then, allow me to show you what I've picked out for you," I said and escorted my client to the cube. "Does this meet with your approval and expectations, or would you like to see the fireman I have in the next room?"

The man looked Officer Reynolds over, licked his lips hungrily and said, "No, this policeman is exactly what I want." With that my client handed me an envelope containing the usual fee for such procurement. Just so there are no misunderstandings allow me to go over the rules again," I said to my client and he nodded in agreement. "The buyer is not allowed to torture or permanently disfigure the object, these being the two big rules you understand."

The client nodded again and I snapped my fingers. Two of my assistants then entered the cube and tied a blindfold over Officer Reynolds' eyes. He fought and twisted, still trying to escape. Some clients will wear a mask because they like to look in their captive's eyes during the encounter, but always their identity is kept safe. We then left the client alone with Officer Reynolds and went upstairs away from the scene that was about to unfold. To be sure that I'm never really far away in case things get out of hand by either one of the persons within the cube, things are always videotaped and if everyone plays by the rules the client can keep the video or destroy it. I never keep anything from these encounters.

While watching the monitor from the office I saw the client enter the cube and shut the door behind him. I saw Officer Reynolds' head turn in the direction the noise came from. You could feel the tension in that little cube as well as it see it when my client came in behind the bound up and blindfolded cop. He jumped him fast and hard, shoving his body up against the glass wall. You could see the cop squirm and struggle, trying to lift his legs, but totally unable to do so due to the chain keeping those legs two and a half feet apart. Officer Reynolds did his best to resist but this was my client's first order that I had filled for him. The helpless cop cursed at him with his body pinned against his assailant and the wall. My client grabbed the officer by his thick black hair and pulled his head back against his shoulder while his other hand slid between the struggling cop's legs

"You are one pretty bitch aren't you Officer?" my client seethed. "I am going to show you what that hot body of yours is good for."

"You fucking son-of-a-bitch faggot," the cop roared through clenched teeth. "You can't do this to me!"

My client simply laughed as he squeezed the struggling officer's cock through his snug fitting uniform slacks.

"I think that inwardly you really like this don't you Officer?" my client teased the captive cop. "In fact from now on I think that we should call you Officer Pussy. What do you think?"

"I like women you fucking freak," the officer responded this time while he continued bucking his body and thrashing in his bindings.

Then, my client unfastened the wall hooks, freeing his plaything's feet but leaving the collar secured to the ceiling. He grabbed the cop by the shoulders and turned him around to face him.

"Now stay right where you are Officer, while I get a good look at you," my client teased.

"Please Mister, just let me go and I won't press charges against you," the officer said, trying a new tactic to bargain for his freedom, without results of course.

My client reattached the ankle cuffs, pulling the officer's legs apart as far as the restraints allowed and his hand began to explore the officer's body, admiring his body and uniform. Officer Reynolds' entire body went rigid as he was forced to allow another man's hands to roam over him, over his young, well-toned muscular form. My client then said to the captured cop, "You know, there really is something about a cop's uniform, with the black polyester slacks that are shiny from the starch and snuggly hugging your hips and awesome ass. I just love the way they feel when I feel a hard body in them."

My client pressed his body completely against the helpless officer, he grinded his crotch against his prize while holding him by the hair and at the same time nibbling his ears and kissing his big neck. My client then started thrusting his hips against his newfound plaything and with every thrust you could hear Officer Reynolds grunt like the very air were being forced from his body. The microphone in the cube picked up every noise made by either occupant, from the demands made by the captor to the pleading of his victim. I saw my client kiss and lick the officer's badge. My client then slowly made his way onto his knees until he was staring directly at the evident bulge in the officer's uniform trousers. His hands reached out and pressed against both of Officer Reynolds' hips.

"Now stay right where you are bitch, or you'll be sorry," my client threatened the captive cop. "Do you understand me Officer?"

The officer slowly nodded, looking beyond miserable behind his blindfold. You could hear the breath the cop sucked in through his teeth as my client's hungry mouth found his hot cock. The officer's body lurched forward from the waist up but only as far as the collar chained to the ceiling would allow while my client's mouth sucked, licked and nuzzled his ever-growing member. After a while my client stood up and started running his hands over the uniformed officer, unbuttoning his uniform shirt and lifting up his t-shirt to begin running his hands over the cop's hard chest and abs.

"Please man, please don't do this, I've got a girlfriend," the officer pleaded. "Why, why are you doing this to me?"

"Why am I doing this to you, you ask?" my client asked the officer in return and kissed him on the cheek, getting a grimace from behind the officer's blindfold. "Do you know how hot you are, pussy? You are one of the sexiest men I've ever seen... and I mean to have a little fun with you, if you must know, so now let's get down to it."

That said, my client unhooked the collar chain and ankle cuffs and pushed the officer a few feet, shoving him face down on the bed. You could see the helpless hottie's fists clenched in his restraints.

"*Please*, please, I'm begging you now man, don't this to me," the cop begged of his assailant.

Of course hearing a hot, helpless cop beg is really a turn-on to me, and I was sure it was a turn-on to my client as well.

My client crawled onto the bed and jumped on top of the cop who started bucking and jerking his body frantically.

"Yeah, that's it, fight me pussy boy, pussy cop, I like it when you pretty bitches give me a run for my money," my client seethed.

You could see the two men as their bodies bucked and squirmed. The client was a very handsome, power driven man of 47 who had a thing about dominating authority figures. Laying atop Officer Reynolds, using his knees to push and keep his victim's legs apart, grinding his cock onto that perfect ass, he was a contented and satisfied client at that moment. His hand reached around his cop victim's hips and between his legs, held onto the hardening bulge found there and squeezed a bit. The officer seethed through clenched teeth and squirmed in misery some more. Then, laying his full body on top of the current object of his desires he reached down and picked up the ring-gag lying on the floor under the bed. He meanly shoved the ring into the officer's mouth and pulled the leather straps tight around the man's neck, tight and secure. You could still hear Officer Reynolds' words as he cursed, cussed and pleaded, but really unable to articulate himself and form words through the open-mouthed gag.

"Now we're gonna see if you're a good cock sucker or not," my client told his new toy.

"*Rhooo!*" the cop cried through the ring gag, trying to scream out the word "no," but of course it fell on deaf ears.

My client got up and walked around to the head of the cot, grabbed the handsome officer by a fistful of hair and pulled his blindfolded face up, exposing his forced open mouth. The client secured the collar around the victim's neck, this time to the metal rail of the cot, thus limiting the poor cop's movement. While holding the cop by the hair the client, with one hand, unzipped his custom made trousers and pulled out a nice sized hard cock and shoved it into the helpless, warm cavity of Officer Reynolds' mouth. The sound of forced slurping was magic in the air. Holding onto a handful of thick, dark hair with one hand and a hard cock with the other the client force-fed the now Officer Pussy a 7 inch thick cut cock. You could see the smile on my client's face as he listened to the gags and gurgles of a ravaged, enraged virgin mouth and throat. This went on for a while until the officer seemed resigned to his fate and current purpose in life. Upon seeing the fight leave the helpless cop from being force-fed my client pulled his hard, wet cock out of Officer Reynolds' mouth and commanded the now Officer Pussy to stick his tongue out and lick the hard offering that was dangling before him. Still holding the cop by the hair he guided the protruded tongue up and down the shaft of his still very hard cock. He pulled Officer Reynolds' head back and ordered him to say "Thank you Sir." He waited a minute and no words were spoken by the ring gagged cop or my client. My client said, "I'm only going to ask you one more time bitch, and if you don't do as you are told, well, I just hope your will is up-to date, now say it!" A few seconds went by as if Officer Reynolds were actually weighing his options when he whispered the words as best he could through his ring gag as he had been commanded.

"Louder bitch," my client instructed and with a shout the helpless officer railed, "Rhank Rhuuu Rir!" trying to say "Thank you Sir!" through the invasive ring gag holding his mouth wide open.

"Thank you for what bitch?" my client demanded.

"Rhank Rhuuu ror rhettin' nee shuck ye rock shur!" the cop voiced, trying to say, "Thank you for letting me suck your cock Sir!"

The cop's words slurred miserably through his clenched teeth and echoed in the small cube he was captive in.

"Now that's a good boy," my client said as he let go of the cop's hair and patted him on the head.

The cop looked up at my client in total anguish...

"We have to wrap this up because I have to be in New York tomorrow," my client said to no one in particular as he walked to the foot of the bed and secured the officer's ankles to the cot legs.

Then, he walked to the side of the bed, sat down and shoved the officer onto his side and unbuttoned and unzipped the tight fitting uniform slacks... and forcibly yanked them down the cop's muscular legs, first one side then the other. Fight had returned to the helpless officer, him cursing yet again through his ring gag, as he no doubt knew what was coming next, but with his collar still secured and his legs bound to the cot-frame as well his struggling only assisted in helping his assailant to remove his uniform slacks over his shoes and socks. The client yanked down the cop's slacks and then his underpants with very little effort. The client then took a few pillows and forced them under the helpless hottie's hips before forcing him to roll onto his stomach. I don't think I've ever seen anything so pretty in my life, the cop's round, firm ass shoved up in the air with his lace-up cop issued shoes and thick black socks still on him. I almost felt sorry for him as I fondled the large, cash-filled envelope. My client then mounted the helpless officer, shoving the officer's legs apart with his knees, which caused the bound buck to squirm and struggle like never before. The screams of anger, fear and revulsion still echoed from his ring-gagged mouth.

"Now to get my money's worth from my new pussy boy," my client said and I could not see from the camera angle, but I knew the minute the officer's ass no longer belonged to him.

The first thrust of my client's hips and the backward thrashing of the officer's head told me that the virgin, hot ass I had acquired was no more.

The client mercilessly fucked the helpless cop for a long while. With each thrust of my client's hips you could see the officer's whole body jerk forward and back. His entire face was clinched, an expression of utter agony, anger and humiliation etched behind his blindfold; his teeth were biting into the ring gag and his fists were knotted until his knuckled had turned white. The sound of a painful grunt accompanied each forceful thrust my client made into the cop's virgin recesses. When finally my client's back arched and he unloaded his essence into the newly acquired dumpsite of a hot ass, his body collapsed on top of the helpless officer's, their bodies side by side, sweat of two hot studs mingled. They were both breathing so heavily that one would have thought that a marathon had just been finished. My client finished, got up and replaced his now spent manhood back into the tailored housing of his suit pants. Sitting on the side of the bed he gently stroked the officer's sweaty, matted hair and said thank you for one sweet ride he would never forget… and with that he pushed the officer onto his side. The cop made no effort at all to thwart my client's intent, but he did let out a miserable sounding moan. My client reached up, grabbed the officer's badge and ripped it off the cop's uniform shirt.

"I think I'll keep this as a little memento of our new friendship," my client laughed.

The officer responded with a weak sounding "mother fucker" through his ring gag but it came out sounding more like, "Rhutter ruckha" as he laid there. My client laughed again and said, "Don't you mean stud fucker?" as he pocketed the badge and then exited the cube.

After making sure that my client was 100 percent satisfied with my latest acquisition and giving directions to return him to his hotel room, I gave orders to clean up and return Officer Reynolds to his life. I did think about using the handsome muscular cop but I really didn't have the heart. I was so fucking horny and about to visit the hot fireman that we had acquired earlier when my assistant informed me that I had a potential client on the phone. I answered the phone and the client was describing to me a very detailed description of the object he wanted me to procure for him. The client turned out to be the 25-year-old son of the client that had just left. He wanted to show his father he was in control and be dominating enough to take over the family business…

I would have to think about this one later… because at the moment I had a fireman that needed his hose inspected…

LETTER TO SPORTSWRITERS

Dear Sportswriters,

Recently I read in the newspapers, on the internet and even in magazines about how Yankee pitcher, Mariano Rivera switched to wearing the "high sock" look with his baseball uniform this season, 2011. I have to say how it amazed and delighted me to see articles and comments in the news about a baseball player's fashion choice where his socks were concerned. In my opinion not enough attention is devoted to this at all. Until I had sent an e-mail to a sportswriter a few years back calling Orlando "El Duque" Hernandez the high-kicking high-socked New York Yankee's Pitcher, I do not think the sportswriter I wrote to ever even thought of him in that context. But yes, Mariano Rivera... As one commentator was quoted as saying, "When you're Mariano Rivera you don't have to explain how you wear your socks with your baseball uniform." I realize that while Mariano Rivera said, "Guy's its just socks," where his new style of wearing his socks high made headlines I was inclined to agree that yes, it's just socks, and to disagree as well, where, well, it's not "just socks."

While it is just socks there really is something to be said about a man who chooses the high sock look, be it in sports or even for the corporate office with his business attire. OTC (over the calf) socks are touted as the proper hosiery for a man to wear when clad in a business suit, for the simple reason that if he happens to cross his leg while in a business meeting, he does not run the risk of showing any leg skin between the top of his sock and his suit trousers. But it is not the office businessman I am here to make note of in this correspondence, at least not this time out.

My name is Christopher Trevor and as a published author of thirty-one books on the subject of "Male Feet" and all things related therein, I feel very qualified to be writing this narrative. As already stated, there is most definitely something to be said for professional baseball players who choose to wear what has come to be called "High Socks" with their uniforms. Pants rolled up knickers style (a style that dates back to the early days of baseball, or as its come to be called nowadays, "old school") with "high" tight socks have become a fashion statement for a host of players out there on the baseball field. Even in neighborhood baseball leagues a lot of the players are opting for this style, as an example "The Brooklyn Cyclones" and as another example, "The Staten Island Yankees." For some reason those tight fitting, dark colored (or red if you are a Red Sox fan) socks add a certain flair and regality to a baseball player's uniform. Chad Curtis, a former slugger for the New York Yankees wore his navy blue "High Socks" so tight that some people were heard to say that they actually looked thin enough to resemble a pair of men's OTC nylon dress socks by Gold Toe brand. In a rare interview concerning his socks and on the subject of baseball players who wear "high socks," Chad Curtis said that he chose that style of socks so that his kids would know which player was him on the field.

Chipper Jones wore his socks "high" and then, as was pointed out to me by a sock watching buddy, after his divorce Mr. Jones went back to the long legged baseball uniforms. Some people in small circles where this sock watching is concerned have wondered if the event of his divorce had anything to do with Chipper Jones ceasing to wear "High Socks." Orlando "El Duque" Hernandez, (who I mentioned at the outset of this narrative) a former pitcher for the New York Yankees is what some of us who love this fashion statement call the "godfather" of the "High Sock" baseball style, reason being that it was he who seems to have started this trend. Orlando "El Duque" Hernandez was also once referred to as the "high kicking", "high socked" El Duque in an article written a while back by sportswriter Mark Hale, after I had e-mailed him on this subject.

Then of course there is the favorite of most sock watcher baseball fans, Doug Mientkiewicz... In an interview Doug called himself a "throwback" sort of player. When asked what he meant by that he said that he bats with no glove and wears "high socks." And who can forget the time when Jason Varitek (while wearing his red "high sox) duked it out on the field with Alex Rodriguez? At that time Alex Rodriguez had not yet himself made the switch to high socks, but we are glad that he did. One of my buddies said "High Socks" rule when it was determined that Jason Varitek had kicked A-Rod's ass... With all this in mind, as I am sure there are many a baseball fan out there who does not give a thought to this "High Sock" fashion trend, but there is a group of us out there that do give it special attention.

I suppose it can be said that we are a group of foot, sock, shoe, and sneaker and even boot enthusiasts. Some of us call ourselves "Foot Friends." There are various websites and YAHOO groups out there that cater to this very, until recently for a lot of us out there, private sort of fascination...

Albert Pujols plays for the Cards and for the most-part favors long legged uniform trousers, but has been seen to wear striped "high socks."

Barry Zito wears stir-ups over his high socks as does Scott Brosius.

Barry Zito, who I happen to think of as the darling of stir-ups once said, "There's something to be said for the "dumb jock", his intelligence doesn't get in the way. I think I'm more aware, so I fight more battles."

Nomar Garciaparra of the Boston Red Sox, like Albert Pujols mostly favors long legged trousers with his uniform but has been seen with red "high socks" from time to time. You go Nomar!

Tim Laker of the Indians falls into this category of "sometimes" wearing his baseball socks "high." Ben Sheets, a ruggedly handsome baseball player looks awesome in his uniform when he chooses to wear navy blue "high socks."

Chad Ogea and Bruce Aven will also fall into the category of players who "sometimes" choose "high socks" with their baseball uniforms, whereas Doug Mientkiewicz, no matter what team he plays for, always seems to favor wearing his socks high.

The baseball player that in my opinion, I would have to say started this entire fascination for me way back in the late 1970s and early 1980s was Mets player Wally Backman. Wally always wore stir-up socks over his high white sweat socks.

Alfonso Soriano is, in my opinion, "El Duque" Junior.

Yankee reliever Jason Anderson is a young and handsome player who thankfully favors "high socks" with his uniform."

Charles Gipson of the Yankees would be considered a hunk in "high socks" when he chooses to wear them as would Dane Bubela of the Braves.

Mike Piazza falls into a category all his own when it comes to good looks. This slugger favors high socks once in a blue moon but when he does he looks simply superb in them.

Todd Zeile of the Mets and Nick Johnson (lastly of the Yankees if I remember correctly) wear their navy blue "high socks" so well and almost like bookends.

Jim Thome is an all-time favorite when it comes to us enthusiasts of high socks.

Tom Seaver sported thin stir-ups over his white sweat socks back in the day as did Tim Teufel.

Roger ("The Rocket") Clemens has been known to wear his socks "high" on occasion and as luck would have it, for some reason he has been questioned about it in interviews. I can only surmise that the interviewer is a sock enthusiast. Roger Clemens has said that at times he wears his socks "high" in honor of "El Duque", his former teammate who always wears his socks in that fashion and when the weather is hot it tends to keep him cooler.

Like Tom Seaver and Tim Teufel, the Angels' Dick Schofield wore thin stir-ups over his white sweat socks. Jamie Moyer also favors stir-ups.

One of the hunkiest and best looking baseball players to sport stir-ups with his thick white sweat socks is John Wetteland. Who could ever forget when the Yankees won the World Series back in 1996 and Joe Girardi hoisted John Wetteland against himself? John Wetteland's legs wrapped around Joe Girardi which really showed off those stir-ups over the heroes thick white sweat socks.

Aaron Boone and Bubba Crosby and Bobby Crosby are a navy blue "high-socked" threesome and bookends, just like Nick Johnson and Todd Zeile.

Manny Ramirez has been seen to wear "high" red sox over his thick white sweat socks.

The Giant's J.T. Snow is a "high-socked" player in a class all his own, handsome, rugged and regal looking in those high socks as he steps out onto the field.

Todd Walker and Jason Tyner also make the "high socks" grade as do Derek Bell and John-Ford Griffin.

A special mention goes out to R.A. Dickey who can't seem to make up his mind where his "high socks" are concerned. He has been seen in red "high sox", navy blue tight fitting "high socks" and navy blue stir-ups with his white sweat socks. As of late since he has joined The New York Mets the slugger seems to favor navy blue "high socks." His bearded unkempt look brings the entire fashion statement together somehow.

Rafael Furcal has been seen in "high" striped socks, which, as pointed out add a whimsical element to the baseball look.

Two of the hottest "high socked" players of the Red Sox, Matt Clement and Jason Varitek not only wear red "high sox" but they each sport a villainous looking goatee.

While on the subject of Red Sox mentions should be made of Mark Bellhorn and Bill Mueller.

Jamey Carroll of The Nationals is a recent and very intense discovery.

Mark Prior of The Cubs is known for his navy blue stir-ups.

Nate Robertson sometimes chooses high socks.

A.J. Burnett, who has come to be known as "The Pie Man" is a ruggedly handsome dark haired guy who used to choose black high socks but as of late has taken to wearing his baseball uniform pants in the long legged style while Athletics outfielder Eric Byrnes chooses green "high socks" with his uniform. Jeromy Burnitz falls into the same category as A.J. Burnett.

Honorable "high sock" mentions go to Junior Spivey, the Blue Jays Reed Johnson, the Brewers Tyler Houston and the Twins' Luis Rivas.

For the most part Robin Ventura chooses long legged pants with his uniform but from time to time the handsome player will opt for navy blue stir-ups.

Pedro Martinez is another player who switches off from time to time to where his "high socks" are concerned.

Kevin Millar and Trot Nixon of The Red Sox both choose red "high socks" with their uniforms.

Vic Darensbourg (the 7th Mets reliever) recently showed a tad of leg skin between his knickers and high socks. That is always sexy somehow when a man does that...

The Bluejay's David Bush is a total hunk in his high socks.

Miguel Cabrera makes this list as does the Orioles Brian Roberts.

Nebraska's Ryan Wehrle wears striped "high socks" while Nebraska's Joe Simokaitis opts for the basic solid colored high sock.

Arizona State's Jeff Lavish and Travis Buck choose high socks with their baseball uniforms.

It seems that the list can go on and on with names such as: Tulane's Nathan Southard.

Heath Bell wears dark thick stir-ups over white sweat socks as opposed to Wally Backman who chose thin stir-ups with his white sweat socks back in the day.

Tennessee's Eli Lorg receives an honorable mention as does Baylor's Michael Griffin, Arizona State's Joey Hooft, Tiger's Brandon Inge and the Cub's Neifi Perez.

When Johnny Damon played for The Boston Red Sox he "sometimes" wore high red socks. Then, when he joined the New York Yankees he at first "sometimes" wore navy blue "high socks" but by the end of his time with the Yankees he had made the switch totally to navy blue high socks.

The most recent mentions of high socked players go out to Curtis Granderson, Oliver Perez, and David Robertson and "sometimes" David Wright chooses high socks, although I am sure we all wish he would choose them all the time... And even more recently I am happy to mention that Nick Swisher of The New York Yankees has recently made the transition to navy blue high socks, just as his buddy A-Rod did various seasons ago at this point. When Andy Petitte came out of retirement to pitch again for the New York Yankees he returned to his "once in a while" style of wearing high socks with his uniform...

SAM'S COMPUTER GLITCH

from inspiration by Christopher
Trevor's executive buddy, Sam

My name is Sam Williams, well; at least for the purposes of this narrative my name is Sam Williams. If my legal name were known I doubt that my contemporaries *and* especially my wife, would never believe what I'm about to relate herein. I was on a business trip in New York City when this happened. Seeing as I'm a married guy and all that good stuff I never thought I would be telling of this, but since I discovered various websites that seem to cater to this sort of thing, well, it just seemed like the story wanted out of me and to be told... or maybe I just can't stop thinking about it. You see, ever since this happened, when I get dressed for work in the morning, well, to be more precise here, when I pull my dark colored nylon over the calf (OTC) dress socks on in the mornings I always spring an erection now... since this happened.

Before this happened my socks was just that, just my socks, or to be more precise, just my dress socks... I mean, I'm just an

ordinary business suited Joe, you know what I mean? Like most
other guys out there my socks are just that, my socks. I recall one
time when I was buying some new Gold Toe brand dress socks in
Macys, I was with my wife and I had picked out about five three-
packs of my usual OTC style in both black and navy blue, not
giving it a thought, you know what I mean? I remember though
also, that on that particular shopping spree a few macho looking
dudes seemed to be watching with rapt attention as I picked out
the dress socks from the racks. I didn't give that a thought either,
until what I want to tell you about in this narrative happened... As
I said, before this happened my socks were just my socks... now
it seems that they're more than just socks... and I'll tell you why
shortly enough.

Let me begin by saying again that for the purposes of this
narrative my name is Sam Williams. I'm 34 years old, I stand tall
at just about six feet two inches, and I have blond executive cut
style hair ala Sam Champion, my namesake (laugh), and dark blue
eyes. I work for a mortgage company in Chicago and every four
to six months part of my job requires me to visit other branches
of the company in other cities. I was in New York City when this
"incident" occurred. To be more precise I was in my hotel room at
the elite and ritzy Diamond Hotel in the heart of Times Square when
this "incident" occurred. My company always puts its executives
up in the best hotels with the very best accommodations, up to and
including computer services if said executive so desires it... or in
my case if said executive requires it, seeing as the computer in my
hotel room wasn't working properly on my first night there that
week.

The Diamond Hotel supplies executives with desktop
computers, the only thing we need to do is bring our software discs.

Well, after I had inserted a disc of current reports,
spreadsheets and e-mail correspondence into the CD ROM drive

of my hotel room computer I was greeted with only one report and was unable to access the rest of what was on the disc. I could not believe it, that's the kind of luck I had been having of late, and I really, REALLY needed to view those reports and have them to my superiors via e-mail ASAP. I hadn't attended two lengthy meetings in one of the hotel's conference rooms that day for nothing after all.

After rebooting the computer numerous times, cleaning the disc and just about everything else computer geeks would advise an executive to do in cases like this I decided to call the hotel desk for assistance.

With my navy blue pinstriped suit jacket draped over a chair, my tie pulled down, the first two buttons of my white button down shirt undone and my shirtsleeves rolled up to just below my elbows, I sat behind the computer desk and called the hotel's front desk.

When the desk clerk on duty that evening answered and asked how he could be of assistance I quickly explained the problem I was having with the hotel computer in my room. The desk clerk apologized profusely and told me that he would have a tech up to my room as quickly as possible. I thanked him, hung up the phone, leaned back in my desk-chair and looked at the computer screen miserably. I had an important meeting to be at in the morning, once again in one of the hotel's conference rooms, and the damned meeting was set for eight AM, which meant that, depending on how long it took the computer geek to get my computer working properly and how long it took me to do what I had to do afterwards I would not be getting much sleep that night.

With a feeling of frustration consuming me I reached forward, grabbed a piece of blank paper from the desktop, crumpled it, and flung it at the computer screen.

"Damn, my old man was right, these things have taken over the world," I muttered and reached down to unlace my wingtips, slid them halfway off to air them and my navy blue socked feet out a bit, seeing as I had been wearing those damned Florsheim's since six AM.

I pressed my Gold Toe socked toes into the back sections of my shoes and swiveled around a bit in my desk chair, wondering how long it would take for the hotel's computer geek to get to my room to service the computer… and worse yet… how long it would take him to get it working properly… and then how long it would take me to finish what I needed to do… I glanced at my watch and saw that it was already nearly nine PM, Jeez!

As luck would have it, it was only ten minutes later when there was a knock at my hotel room door. I extracted my socked feet the rest of the way out of my wingtips, kicked the shoes to the side of the desk and dashed to the door. My socks had drooped down a bit during the day, as happens to most executive's socks and I hadn't paid any attention to it, hell, it was something I was used to having happen on a daily basis after all… but I had no idea of just how much it would mean to the computer geek, once he got started working on my computer that is.

"Who is it?" I called out.

"My name is Steve Schwartz Sir, I was sent up to service your computer," was the reply I heard from the other side of the door.

"Ah good, good," I replied and quickly opened the door.

The young man named Steve was about five feet nine inches tall, give or take: he had brown eyes, brown short cut hair and was dressed in the regal looking uniform of a hotel bellman. I supposed that besides being a bellman he moonlighted as a computer geek as well, or the hotel simply required all its employees to wear the uniform. But to tell it plainly I would not have cared if the twenty-something looking guy was a construction worker, just as long as he was able to get my computer working properly.

Steve wheeled in a small cart that contained an array of computer looking gadgetry.

"Mr. Williams?" he asked, his hand held out.

"That's me, good to see you here Steve," I replied and shook hands with him.

"I'm sure I'll have your computer working in just about no time Sir," Steve said as he shook hands with me, his grip strong and tight, and a real man's hearty handshake.

"That's good to hear, that is really good to hear, seeing as I want to finish up what I need to do and then try to get some sleep before my meeting tomorrow morning," I said as the guy continued pumping my hand with his.

"Then let me get started Sir," Steve said, let go of my hand and wheeled his cart over to the desk where the computer was as I closed and locked the door behind him.

I watched as he sat down at the desk and pressed a host of keys on the keyboard that brought up the "My Computer" options. After perusing the options and clicking on various icons he then clicked on the "Start" key and perused the listing of programs that the computer in my room was presently running.

"Hmm, I'm not seeing anything the matter from here Sir," Steve said and stood up.

He stepped to his cart and picked up a square gizmo that had a wire attached to it. At the end of the wire was what looked like some sort of adaptor plug-in attachment. That's really the best way I can describe what it was that Steve had picked up from the cart. As I already pointed out I'm no computer geek… I'm just a guy who uses computers, when it comes to programming and all that tech stuff I'm totally in the dark.

"Being that I can't find anything wrong with your computer from the desktop Sir, I'll have to run a test on the tower under your desk," Steve explained, holding up the attachment he had in hand.

"Sounds like a plan to me," I said, tugging at my pulled down tie, a nervous tic of mine I suppose you could say.

"Okay, what this is, is a Iomega HDD, external F drive, what I'm going to do is hook it up to your tower and save everything that's on the hard-drive of the hotel computer, and whatever programs you're running from your disc," Steve explained.

I shrugged my broad shoulders and chuckled.

"What I'll need for you to do Mr. Williams is for you to sit at the desk and press the keys on the keyboard that I indicate while I'm working on the tower under your desk," Steve said, glancing down at the floor and stealing a glance or two at my navy blue silk-socked feet, a look or two at the moment that was lost on me.

I mean, being that he worked as a computer geek for executives in a posh and ritzy hotel the guy must have seen countless executives with their shoes off and in their socked feet, right? I would soon find out otherwise…

"Okay, no problem at all," I said as Steve licked his lips, shucked off his hotel uniform jacket, took off his bowtie and then hunkered down by the desk, draping his jacket over the back of the desk chair and depositing his bowtie in the jacket pocket.

He slowly worked his way under the big desk-well space, fitting easily underneath it.

I'm sure he was glad that the hotel provided oversized desks for their executive guests…

Once Steve was under the desk and tinkering with the computer tower I hiked my suit trousers up a bit at the knees before sitting down, not thinking how in doing so that it would really show off even more of my navy blue dress socks… my drooping down silk navy blue dress socks by Gold Toe… to be utterly precise here after all…

"Okay, the Iomega HDD F drive is hooked up to your computer tower Mr. Williams," Steve called out from under the desk.

"Okay, just let me know what you need for me to do from up here," I said down to him, sliding only halfway in against the desk, my fingers positioned and ready above the keyboard.

"Uh, yes, in a moment Sir, I just need to get this device properly hooked up now down here," Steve said, indicating the Iomega HDD F drive, suddenly sounding a little unsure of himself.

As I heard the device he had been holding in his hand, the Iomega HDD external F drive to be exact, being plugged into and worked into a section of the computer tower I asked him if he was okay, noting how his voice pattern had suddenly changed, actually it was a tad breathless sounding.

"Uh, yes Mr. Williams, I'm okay," Steve said. "It's just that, uh, well, I... I better get to work down here."

He reached forward for a second, gave one of my socked feet a squeeze and then he was puttering around with the computer tower. I didn't comment (yet) on the fact that he had just squeezed one of my navy blue socked feet.

"Okay, so far everything is registering okay with the external hard drive Mr. Williams, now, if you would just click on the "Start" icon and then click on "My Computer" I would really appreciate it," Steve said from below the desk.

"Sure thing," I responded, leaned forward a bit and without giving it any thought I hefted my feet up a bit and pressed my Gold toes against the carpet.

I guided the "mouse" over the computer screen and clicked on the icons that Steve had requested I click on.

"Okay, now tell me Mr. Williams, do you see on the screen all of your files and programs that the PC should be running?" Steve asked from under the desk, his voice quavering a bit.

"Uh, just the couple I saw earlier when I first tried to use the PC and…" I began, but then my words were cut short when I felt Steve's hand encircle my right foot as it was propped up on my gold toes. "Ulp… so uh, as you can see, or maybe you can't… there are a lot more things on the disc that I need to be able to access and…"

But as I spoke Steve lifted my right foot from the floor and gripping it tight as all hell stretched it out so that my leg was in a totally prone position now.

"Uh Steve, what uh, what all are you…" I sputtered and stammered.

"I'll get back to your PC in a bit Mr. Williams," Steve said, holding my foot in two hands now, his face so close to it I saw as I glanced down in awe at him. "Your uh, your socks are scrunched down a bit."

"Yeah, uh, that happens a lot to executives like me, comes from stomping around in our wingtips all day and…" I explained, sounding totally stupid to myself.

I mean, what in all hell was the guy doing holding my foot in his hands for and his face was close enough to kiss it if he wanted to? But then, I got the further shock of my life as the guy hefted my foot a tad more, pulled my sock up for me and then, oh God, and then, he did kiss my foot, *fuck*, the computer tech geek kissed my damned socked foot.

I watched in a state bordering on trauma of some sort as the guy then held my foot aloft by the heel with one hand and around my gold toes with the other hand, and he leaned his head down and planted delicate almost loving kisses all over the top section of my foot.

"Oh holy shit…" I muttered and found myself falling back in my chair, lounging almost.

My robust chest jutted out a bit under my white button down shirt and I gripped the arms of the chair. At the sight of the computer geek holding my socked foot aloft and kissing it, *fucking kissing it*, my cock sprung *instantly* to attention and I found myself in the throes of a feeling of ecstasy I had never known before.

Sitting there, totally riveted to the chair it seemed I then watched as the computer geek pressed his nose against the gold toes section of my foot... and he sniffed and inhaled heartily, *oh God!* As he inhaled my foot stink he squeezed my foot tighter yet, lovingly, almost obsessively. I found myself taking deep gasping breaths as the guy sniffed and snuffed at my socked toes and caressed and kneaded my foot in his strong grip.

"Oh God Steve... what are you... what are you doing to me here?" I murmured breathlessly.

But Steve did not reply, instead he simply went on sniffing at my socked toes, inhaling their leathery and nylon and feet stink odors. To my disbelief he stuck out the tip of his tongue and lapped and licked a bit at my socked toes. I felt a mixture of ecstasy and outright chills as they consumed my body. Never before had I seen, nor allowed a guy to be holding onto my foot and sniffing and kissing it the way Steve the computer geek was doing at the moment. I had to admit that the feelings as he massaged, squeezed, kneaded and planted kisses on my socked foot all combined felt beyond awesome. My hard and erect cock in my suit trousers was testament to that.

When I looked down under the desk again I nearly flew out of my chair, because the guy was slowly and methodically taking the toes section of my socked foot into his mouth, as much as possible it seemed.

"*Oh God,*" I groaned as I felt his sucking action then, as he sucked at my socked toes, drinking all the sock juice out of the gold material.

I gripped the arms of the chair tighter and looked and stared at the guy in awe, unable to speak for the moment. Holding my foot in hand and in mouth Steve looked up at me from under the desk, for all of a second. He grinned wickedly around my socked toes that were encased in his craw, as if what he was doing to me, to my socked foot, was all normal and status quo. He didn't seem the least bit worried that I might report him to the hotel management for sniffing my socked toes, chowing on them and massaging and caressing my socked foot. It was when he saw how tented my suit trousers were at the crotch that an even greater glee came over the computer geek's face, and that seemed to give him the signal from me that it was okay for him to continue... and continue he did buds, continue he did.

I found myself gasping and grunting then as the guy next was planting kisses and smooches on the top part of my foot as he held it in his hands. Looking under the desk I watched, still in a state of awe as he dribbled onto my foot as he held it tight by the heel and socked toes and then sucked up his saliva. The feelings in the topmost part of my socked foot as he sucked on it were unbelievable... and I swear I felt it in my cock, my cock that was stiffening more and more and engorging like a thing alive in my suit trousers.

"Steve, my computer, please man," I whimpered breathlessly as the guy then gently kissed the tips of my socked toes, sending more chills and thrills through my very being.

"I'll get to it Mr. Williams, all in due time Sir, first things first," Steve said and positioned himself even further under my desk-well.

Once he was positioned against the back panel of my desk-well Steve lifted my socked foot by the heel and toes so that the bottom of it was staring him in the face...

"Nice, so nice, beautiful socked feet Mr. Williams, so beautiful," Steve whispered as he trailed the fingertips of one of his hands up and down and up and down the bottom of my socked foot.

As he rubbed his fingers gingerly over and over the bottom of my socked foot he gently kissed the balls of it, inhaling deeply my leather mixed with nylon mixed with feet stink odors.

"*Oh* yeah, my boss sure as all fucks sent me to the right room tonight Mr. Williams," Steve purred under the desk, his nose pressed against the bottom of my socked foot.

As he worked on my foot that was under the desk with him I pressed the gold toes section of my other foot firmly and hard against the carpet where I was seated. By then my cock was huge and ready for takeoff like a goddamned rocket on the launching pad in my suit pants…

But then, all coherent thoughts were suddenly cut off and I screamed in a man's passion as Steve stuck out his tongue… and slithered it slowly up and down the bottom of my foot.

"*AWWW* man, that's awesome Steve," I bellowed.

"Glad to hear you're enjoying it Mr. Williams," Steve whispered huskily and he again and again trailed his tongue up and down the bottom of my socked foot.

"*AWWW* man, fuck, that feels so good," I murmured and leaned back in the desk chair, my head lolling back as I panted and looked up at the ceiling.

"The bottom of your socked foot is oh so soft and delectable Mr. Williams," Steve said, sounding sexy as hell as he then held my foot tight by the center of it with two hands and rubbed and caressed it over his face a few times.

"Tell me Steve, do you perform these foot and sock services for all the executive guests here at the hotel?" I asked my foot benefactor breathlessly.

"No way Mr. Williams, only the hot ones who wear Gold toe OTC socks," Steve replied, grinning up at me from under my desk. "Now, with that in mind Mr. Williams, let's see if your socks are OTC at that…"

That said Steve hiked my suit trousers up, up and up my leg until it was bunched around my knee, revealing that yes, I was indeed wearing OTC Gold toe socks…

"*Oh yes*, oh fuck yes, fucking A," Steve panted and held my leg straight out, gripping it tighter than tight at the calf and the ankle.

Steve then pressed his nose and mouth against the side of my socked calf and began deeply inhaling, sniffing like crazy and kissing and trailing his tongue over and over and over my OTC navy blue nylon dress sock.

"Mr. Williams, fuck yes, yes Sir," Steve reeled under the desk and then began nipping at my socked calf as if he were eating an ear of corn.

"*YUUUUHHH*," I garbled, the sensations of what he was now doing feeling unnerving to me as chills and shrills sped through my entire body. "*Oh God* man… never knew that my damned socks could turn someone on so much… *so much… YUUUHHH…*"

I grinded the toes of my other socked foot harder and harder into the plush carpet, gripped the arm of the desk chair tight with one hand and yanked at my tie with the other hand, pulling my tie down further, unbuttoning more buttons of my shirt, needing air, gasping, grunting, my cock pre-seeding in my suit trousers… oh my word, what an evening it had turned out to be for me…

And at that point Steve reached forward and hooked a hand around my other foot…

Grabbing my other foot by the socked ankle Steve pulled it toward him from his spot under the desk that I was still seated in front of, me having become his foot captive of sorts in a way, seeing as I felt rooted to the chair. Fuck, I couldn't have moved if I wanted to. The way the guy was doing what he was doing to my socked foot, soon to be both my socked feet, with his mouth and tongue and teeth was sending me into a tailspin, and I felt that if I did move, well, I could easily lose my balance buds.

As my first socked foot rested in Steve's lap, remnants of his saliva glistening on it, Steve went to work on my other foot, inspecting it in a way at first as he held it by my arch and toes section.

"Oh man, just as beautiful as your other socked foot Mr. Williams," Steve muttered and then grinned a bit as he proceeded to hike up my suit trouser on that leg as well, up to my knee, revealing all of my OTC sock. "But this sock seems to have drooped a bit on your sexy calf…"

Still grinning Steve did the honors of pulling and hiking my sock up for me till it was straightened and resting good and tight just under my knee.

"There you go Sir, that's better, no executive, especially one of your stature should be with his socks falling down his legs," Steve said and slurped at my socked toes once more.

"*YUHHH, oh man,* yes, yes, you're right Steve, whatever you say bud," I gasped anew as the guy was again sending shrilling thrills through me via my socked feet. "*Aw* man never knew that my socked feet could be so sexually sensitive…"

"Stick with me Mr. Williams and I'll show you just what these sexy socked feet of yours are capable of feeling and making you feel," Steve said and I watched in a state of awe as he next pulled the gold material of my second foot a few inches away from my wiggling toes and slurped that material into his mouth, his lips wrapped reverently and lovingly around it.

"My God," I whispered and I swear I could feel my nipples tingling on my chest as the guy sipped the gold material of my socks like it was a straw he had wedged between his lips and held my foot aloft at his mouth with his hands wrapped tightly and possessively around it, sending me into a state of total ecstasy.

Steve sucked more of my sock into his mouth and his jaws clenched inward, his eyes closed in ecstasy it seemed as he drank the sweat and sock juice from the silky material, driving me crazier and crazier it seemed…

Fuck, I had forgotten all about my computer glitch by then… all I wanted was more and more and more of this wonderful tech servicing and paying homage to my damned socked feet.

A few moments later Steve was holding both my feet in his hands, my legs stretched out and close together as I sat there watching, watching as the guy was now strumming his lips and tongue over and over my socked toes, playing them as if they were a piano…

Oh my word, he held my socked feet tight by the centers of them, his fingers wrapped tightly around them, as if he would *never* let go of them… and just to mention, my suit trousers were still hiked up to my knees, *gawd*, looking down at that I felt like a baseball player who chooses what has come to be called the "High Sock" look with his baseball uniform.

As Steve proceeded to then hold both my feet in front of his face and alternately lick the bottoms of them up and down and up and down I found myself *again* leaning back in my desk chair, lounging practically, as the fucking sock fetishist worked his magic…

He licked and lapped at the bottoms of my feet (the bottoms of my socked feet that is, the bottoms of them seeming to be his favorite spots on my tootsies) as if he was licking a huge lollipop. He held my feet tight by the toes section, spit on the bottoms of them a few times, (I swear his saliva felt so warm as it was pelted against the bottoms of my socked feeties, *AWWW* man…) and then as his saliva dripped slowly down the bottoms of my socked feet he lapped it up, sucking at my feet bottoms, driving me further into a state called Frenzy. My eyes rolled in my head and my lips quivered as I whispered the guy's name, Steve, over and over and over...

A short while later I found myself kneeling on the king-sized bed in the luxury suite of my hotel room, my socked feet and calves dangling down and off the side of the bed. For the slightest of moments I did not even recall how I had gotten from the desk chair to the bed, but then, as Steve knelt behind me and began again licking and lapping at my dangling socked feet, him holding onto them *so tight* by the ankles, it came back to me in a flash. Steve had released his hold on my socked feet and had scurried out from under my desk, pushing me back on my desk chair with the wheels on it, rolling me toward the bed, pressing on my knees to move me and the chair along. As he rolled me toward the bed Steve ordered me to keep my socked feet hoisted up off the floor, not wanting any dust lint to get on them I supposed, seeing as they were nice and moist with his saliva all over them. The computer tech/geek expertly transferred me from my chair to the bed and within what seemed like seconds I was kneeling on the bed, my arms at my sides, my chest puffed out ala military style almost.

Once Steve had me positioned on the bed in the way he wanted he reached around me, hugging me, hugged me against himself and I looked down to see that the guy was undoing my belt, then slowly sliding it out of the loops of my suit pants.

"Steve, what..." I began breathlessly. "I'm, I'm a married guy dude..."

"No worries Mr. Williams, it's still just your socked feet that I'm trolling for here," Steve reassured me and reached up to give my tie a few friendly tugs. "I'm just getting you a tad more comfy for what I want next..."

So instead of stopping the guy I watched, and I watched, and my cock twitched as I watched, looking downward as Steve's hands and fingers moved expertly and at what seemed like bionic speed as he undid my belt, next he undid the fastener on my suit pants and then rolled those suit pants right down my long legs and off me, tossing them onto the bed.

"*Oh man…*" I groaned as I knelt there now in my shirt with my tie askew and pulled down, my white silk executive style tight briefs and of course my OTC navy blue nylon dress socks, DAMN, those socks being the prize that Steve so coveted.

At that point in time I had completely forgotten about my PC issues… From behind me I could feel Steve drinking in the sight of my hard butt cheeks encased in my silk briefs, but then, the guy squatted down behind me at my dangling socked feet, gripped them tight by the ankles and began working his mouth magic on them yet again. He began by gently and delicately planting kisses on the tops of my upturned socked heels… His lips must have been electric because I could feel the current grinding upwards from my heels into my calves and up and down the backs of my legs as the guy went on and on squeezing my socked ankles, strumming his thumbs along my socks and kissing, kissing and kissing the tops of my heels.

I grabbed my necktie with two hands, squeezed it tight and muttered a guttural "*Aw man, Steve,*" and my cock, hard as steel in my silk briefs dribbled and trickled dollops of pre seed like gangbusters…

After my heels had been thoroughly kissed and shown so much love and devotion Steve continued holding tight to my socked ankles and then began trailing the tip of his tongue up and down the bottoms of my socked feet, causing me to curl my toes in the gold sections of my socks… *fuck*… I grabbed my tie with one hand then and moved the palm of my other hand under my button down shirt, grabbing and tweaking my nipples alternately as the fucking computer tech wreaked havoc on my cock via my damned socked feet. My head hung down and I panted crazily…

Kneeling behind me Steve then gripped my socked feet at the toes and worked the bottoms of them like a madman. He trailed his tongue up and down the bottoms of my feet, kissed the bottoms of them over and over and sucked at the balls of them, spitting on them a few times and sucking up his saliva, just as he had done when he was under the desk earlier.

"*Oh* man, Mr. Williams, your feet are awesome Sir," Steve breathed behind me, sniffing heavily at my socks as he worshiped the daylights out of them.

I leaned my head down further and gripped my tie tighter and tweaked my nipples harder and *fucking* reveled in what the guy was doing to me…

I swear, I felt as if I could cum right then and there, right there into my expensive silk briefs, just from the guy cooking my socked feet with his mouth, lips and tongue. I swear, even without my cock being touched I thought I could shoot a whopper of a load of ball juice.

"The bottoms of an executive's OTC socks are the best Mr. Williams," Steve muttered behind me as he held tight to my ankles and was next kissing the undersides of my socks, all the way up the backs of my calves, slithering his tongue along them in between kissing them. "They're so soft and they smell and taste great after a harried executive has been stomping around all day in them in his wingtips or his loafers or his cap toes…"

"*Oh* yeah, I really do stomp at that Steve," I murmured breathlessly. "My God, never had a dude so worked up and so unnerved by my socked feet… of all things…"

As Steve trailed his tongue up and down the undersides of my tall socks he ran his hands up and down them as well, caressing my calves, fuck, I could feel tears of ecstasy welling in my eyes… this was all just too much buds…

"*AWWW,* fuck yeah, yeah," I found myself bellowing, ranting and grunting about a half hour later, a half hour later after still having had my socked feet totally worshiped. "*Fuck* Steve, I'm shooting my load here, right into my damned executive briefs… *YUUUHHH*… and all because you worked me over at my socked feet bud…"

"*Oh yeah,* your socked feet made my night Mr. Williams," Steve said from behind me, playfully snapped the elastic in both my socks and slowly and finally got to his feet…

At eleven thirty PM Steve was done fixing my PC and I had managed to retrieve all the necessary information I would need for the meeting in the morning…

As Steve left my hotel room I stood by the door shaking his hand, thanking him, me barefoot, because in Steve's other hand were my navy blue OTC socks that he had just worshiped and when he had finished he ceremoniously relieved my feet of them, claiming them as his prize and souvenir… of me…

A BET TOO FAR

by Jeff Storm

I had known Blake since we were little kids. We had gone to high school together, gone to the same college, and I had even been his best man at his wedding with Lisa. We both ended up at the University of Florida, but he ended up an accountant and I was a manager of an information technology company. I'd only been in Tampa for a few months, but he'd been here for more than a year.

Now, four years after he had gotten married, Lisa was leaving him. Blake kept calling me and leaned on me some for support, he said. For the most part I didn't mind, but it did seem like he was getting a little clingy. He wanted me and wanted me and wanted me to introduce him to some women to "get his mind off Lisa." Blake was a good looking guy. He was five feet eight inches tall, one hundred and seventy pounds, muscular, worked out, had blonde hair and blue eyes and like me, he was in his late twenties. He could easily score with women if he wanted to, and to be honest he didn't need my help.

Now Blake didn't know that I was gay, and I wanted to tell him, but there never seemed to be a good way to reveal this to him. And now that he was involved in this nasty divorce with Lisa, this did not seem like the time to lay something that heavy on him. Hey, at least they didn't have any kids. Here we were both still dating and he kept asking me why I had never married. Like a lot of gay people would respond I said that I had never found the right person. Blake said to me, "Jeff, I thought I had met the right person, but there are some things that Lisa just won't do for me." I was never sure where to go with that, and I didn't want to know in some ways. I wanted to keep Blake as a friend and as good friends as we had been, we never discussed sex, and I'm sure that's what he meant.

Here it was Saturday afternoon. I got the call I knew was coming. Blake asked me if he could come over and just hang out. He said maybe we could watch the game together and then go out to the bars. My roommate was out of town, so I said sure, TV's open but that I did invite another friend over too. It was University of Florida versus Florida State. We had both grown up in Texas, but we had both ended up at UF. So it was Gators all the way for us. It was kind of weird being in Florida now. It was fall, but still warm, not exactly football weather. Blake came over wearing shorts and a tee shirt. I was in my shorts and a polo shirt- standard wear for my weekend. I wore enough monkey suits during the week, so I wanted to relax on the weekends.

He asked who else was coming over to watch the game. I told him that I still didn't know enough people in Tampa, so it was just us and one other guy that I had just recently met who lived across the hall.

"Fine," Blake said. "Make sure there are enough nachos for me."

He immediately tore into some of the chips and I told him that the guy from across the hall was named Tony. What I didn't tell Blake was that I'd met Tony at one of the local gay bars and had recognized him as a neighbor. I also didn't tell him that I thought Tony was hot. Tony was about five feet eleven inches tall, one hundred and ninety pounds, maybe around the age of thirty or so, and had a hot muscular body. I had seen him in his tee shirt at the bar, but I could easily have imagined him shirtless. He had a hot looking butt as well, and I could imagine myself fucking the hell out of him. I wasn't sure what Tony did for work, but I was thinking that he could be a hot bottom for me.

I'd long ago learned that I liked topping muscle boys, usually muscle boys younger than me. Tony was a little at the high end of my range, but he looked so muscular and hot. I have black hair, brown eyes, stand in at five feet ten inches tall, I'm one hundred and ninety pounds of rock hard muscle and I've been told I'm very handsome. I knew that I could get guys whenever I wanted. I was concerned though that Blake might realize that Tony and I were interested in each other, or at least that I was interested in Tony. I had met Tony just the night before at the local gay bar that I just mentioned. I had recognized him as my neighbor and mentioned the football game. I mentioned also that it'd be me and a straight buddy watching the game, but if he wanted he could come over. He laughed when he told me, "Don't worry Jeff, I won't give you away." I wasn't worried Tony would come across as gay, but I was worried that Blake might notice I was interested in him. But I wanted Tony bad enough so I was willing to risk it.

I had been a UF fan long enough that it never occurred to me to ask Tony if he was a UF or FSU fan. I heard the knock that afternoon and opened the door. Tony looked hot in his gym shorts and tee shirt, but then I saw the FSU logo on his tee shirt.

"Oh man Tony, you're an FSU fan?!?" I asked as he barged his way in.

"Yep, yep Jeff, I went there all four years," Tony said. "That's where I got my degree, and now I'm a lawyer."

I pointed at my UF tee shirt and told him, "Well, it's too bad you have to lose then."

Tony laughed and said, "You may have had a few good years there a while back, but it's our turn this year."

Just then Blake came over to us and said, "Man, I didn't think Seminoles were allowed in this house."

Tony just smiled and introduced himself to Blake.

The game was about to start so I got it all set and we all sat down and started to watch. Blake suggested we bet some money on the game, perhaps twenty dollars each. Tony said he didn't have a lot of money right now, due to student loans, and didn't want to bet money. Me, I couldn't resist, so I asked him what we could bet on then. Tony said, "Well, maybe the losing team has to do whatever the winning team says for two hours." I thought about this. Our team was favored by seven points. I looked over at Blake as if to ask him what he thought. Blake asked Tony, "What do you mean by anything? You mean like housework, cleaning up and stuff?" In response Tony said, "Well, anything. It has to be a forfeit. It could be something embarrassing, like wearing a stupid sign or something." Blake mulled a few seconds and then said, "You do realize that if you lose that you will have two people telling you to do stupid stuff?"

Tony smiled and said, "Look, it's just a friendly wager." With that Blake looked at me and asked, "Are you game?" I looked at Tony and I have to admit that I was thinking that maybe this just might be my chance to get to see his muscular body. I could ask him to strip as part of the "stupid stuff!" I said, "Why not? Okay, you're on."

Just then the kickoff started. There was some beer flowing between the three of us, some nachos, and some snacks. The score was 20-17 in favor of UF at the halftime. Blake said to Tony, "You're going down" and Tony simply smirked and said, "We're the comeback kings. You know that. You're going to clean my apartment, and you're going to like it." I quickly chimed in, "Tony, you'll be cleaning this place up, but in your underwear, oh how embarrassing!" Smiling, Blake looked at me and said, "Yeah, in your underwear Tony."

Tony looked over at us and said, "Oh yeah, well, you'll both be cleaning my place bare assed naked, buck assed naked, totally naked." With that, all of a sudden, we all quieted down as the third quarter started.

20-17 was a little close for me. All of a sudden I was becoming concerned about Tony making Blake and I strip at the same time. I'd never seen Blake naked, and wasn't sure this was a good idea after all, especially if I was going to come out to him later. I just kept praying through the third and fourth quarters that we kept our lead.

I was lucky. We kept our lead all through the third quarter, ending up 27-17 in our favor. We were holding them. The fourth quarter went well for us, until the very end. They scored two touchdowns in the last five minutes of the game. The last touchdown was almost the entire length of the field, and was with seconds to go. It ended up 31-27 in FSU's favor. I couldn't believe this, and neither could Blake. I could tell that he was stunned too. He looked over at me and said, "No way Jeff." I simply shook my head. Tony was smiling from ear to ear and said, "Man, we've been waiting years for a game like that." Damn, he looked so smug that I almost wanted to punch him. Suddenly I remembered the bet. Oh fuck, I thought, maybe he'll forget about that while I get poor Blake out of here.

I said, "Blake, don't you need to get home soon?"

He didn't get it and looked at me as if puzzled.

"No, I can hang around," Blake replied. "We need to go out and meet some ladies anyways."

Then, Tony added, "Besides, I need you both to pay up." I looked at Tony and said, "Well, I got us into this mess, so let Blake go home and you can take your forfeit out on me." Tony chuckled meanly and said, "Nope, you both made the bet, and you'll both pay up. First, let's go to my place. I think it needs some cleaning."

"You're not really going to make us pay up are you?" I asked. "I wouldn't have made you Tony."

"No, you would have made me pay up Jeff," Tony said smugly. "Now, both of you, over to my apartment.

We dutifully marched over to his apartment, just mere steps from mine. Tony opened the door and we were surprised at how neat it already was.

"Man, well, at least it won't take too long to clean up," I said.

"That's right," Tony said. "So now remember how you threatened to make me clean your place in my underwear?"

I looked at Blake and said, "We were just kidding about that Tony." I smiled.

Tony did not look amused, and poor Blake was starting to look worried.

"No, you weren't kidding Jeff," Tony stated sternly. "You would have had me cleaning your apartment in my underwear. I could tell. So let's see how you guys look cleaning my apartment. We'll start out easy. Both of you take off your shoes and socks.'

Feeling totally dismayed I said, "Come on Tony."

Tony simply pointed at my shoes and socks and made a gesturing motion.

"You can put them over by that closet," Tony said.

Feeling miserable I took my shoes and socks off and started putting them over by the closet. As I did so I saw Blake looked a little concerned.

"It'll just be a little embarrassing," I said, trying to reassure him, but I wasn't so sure.

Tony pointed to my shirt and said, "Okay, your shirts can go over by your shoes and socks." I took my shirt off and tried not to look at Blake as he took his off as well. Blake had a smooth chest, as opposed to my somewhat hairy chest. I thought that perhaps he shaved it. That's not too straight behavior I was thinking at that point.

"Okay boys, you ready?" Tony asked, him smiling way too much for my taste. "Pants off now and over by the shirts."

I reluctantly pulled off my khaki shorts and Blake pulled his gym shorts off. We both looked a little concerned and pissed off, but we still played along and put them by the other clothes. I was in my grey boxer briefs. Blake had on some tighty whitey briefs and I have to admit that he looked pretty hot, better than I had expected him to look.

I turned around just in time to see Tony snap a picture of me in my boxer briefs. He did the same thing to Blake.

"Hey, come on, that's not fair," I said.

"All's fair in a bet," Tony said snidely. "Remember Jeff, you and Blake agreed to anything I wanted for two hours. It's only been twenty minutes. Now Jeff, remove those boxer briefs and give me a big smile as I take your picture buck naked."

"Come on Tony, I would never have done something like this to you," I pleaded.

"Hell yeah you would have," Tony countered. "Now smile as you lower those boxer briefs. I need a reminder of the time my naked neighbor boy cleaned my house. Come on Jeff, you're not going to chicken out now, are you?"

With that kind of challenge, I got mad and took off my boxer briefs, quickly. The next thing I knew Tony was snapping a picture of me buck naked.

"Now turn around and let's get a shot of that hot ass of yours Jeff," Tony said.

I turned around in shock to see him grinning at me.

So, with that I turned around and showed my butt to him. I heard the clicking and asked him, "You happy now Tony?"

"Yeah, I'm happy Jeff, because now it's Blake's turn," Tony said. "And you're staying naked Jeff, you hear me?"

Damn, I had tried to move slowly to my clothes, but his comment cut me off. I was kind of curious to see if Blake was going to agree to take off his tighty whities. At the moment I was the only one naked and I was really feeling it.

"Come on Tony, you don't really want to see me naked do you?" Blake almost begged.

"Hell yeah, I do Blake, now, off with the tighty whities and smile for the camera," Tony ordered.

Blake looked fucking hot as he peeled off his tighty whities and his dick sprang into full view. Tony clicked a few pictures of him. I noticed that Blake's dick was hardening up. Hmm, this was becoming interesting.

"Yeah Blake, now turn around and let me see that hot ass of yours," Tony ordered next and Blake did as he was told. "Oh yeah, that's a hot fucking ass!"

I could see Blake blushing as he faced me, his dick jutting out some and his ass pointed at Tony with the camera.

"Now Blake, we're going to have some fun," Tony said. "Put your knees down in front of that couch and bend over the cushion seats.

Blake looked back at Tony in horror.

"Come on Blake, *you* promised to do anything I said for two hours. Now do it. Remember I have naked pictures of you already.

With that Blake started looking very nervous but he bent over the couch. I have to admit his ass looked really hot, and I was boning up now. Tony laughed and said, "Yeah Blake, hot ass, and look, your friend Jeff has boned up just watching you." I turned beet red, totally embarrassed. I couldn't say it wasn't true, but I couldn't have imagined seeing it like this. Tony stripped off his shirt and he had a hot hairy chest, very muscular as well. Then he unzipped his jeans and took them off. He had on boxers with a big hard-on poking out of them.

He came up behind Blake and started lubing up his hole, "*holy shit!*" Blake jumped and exclaimed, "Oh no, please don't!" begging. With that Tony started playing with Blake's nips and was even fingering his hole. Damn, I boned up real big, as Tony then said, "Yeah Blake, looks like Jeff loves seeing your hot booty played with, not to mention your tits. Did you know that I met him at a fag bar?" With that I went beet red.

Next, Tony slapped a pair of handcuffs on Blake and said, "Yeah, I got me a straight boy slut slave now. Poor Blake looked like he was panicking by then and was fighting the handcuffs.

"Come on Tony, Blake *is* straight, just let him go," I pleaded.

"Hell no Jeff, I'm going to play with this straight boy butt, and then I get to watch you do him the way you've always wanted to do him," Tony said meanly. "*And* I'm going to videotape that as well."

I looked and felt horrified. Then I looked over at Blake and he was looking at me like he could not believe any of this and how it had all turned out. But I saw that his dick was still hard.

"Here, let me show you how it's done Jeff," Tony stated and with that, he placed his dick directly at the entrance to Blake's hole.

He lubed up and slid on a condom and then, to mine and Blake's disbelief, he began inching his way in. Blake's eyes crossed in his head and he looked like he was going to pass out. Tony started pushing his way all the way in at that point, slapping Blake's ass cheeks as he went. Poor Blake cried out miserably but he was still conscious. But then, to Blake's dismay Tony started to thrust and push in and out in a rhythmic motion. Blake was moaning and crying some, but I noted that his dick was *still* hard.

As he fucked Blake Tony reached around the guy and toyed with his nips, quite hard too. Blake looked down, saw what Tony's fingers were doing with his nips and the guy looked stunned. But then, to my utter disbelief I saw Blake start to buck his hips against Tony as the guy fucked him.

"Yeah, that's it straight boy," Tony chortled meanly. "Take my dick."

That's when I noticed the red light in the wall. Fuck, I didn't want to say anything to alarm Blake, but Tony *was* indeed filming this. Jesus Christ, he was fucking his conquests, and we were two of them. That's when it happened.

"Get over here Jeff," Tony ordered. "You want a piece of this hot ass don't you boy? I see how hard your dick is.

"No, no, please," Blake said, turning and looking at me pleadingly.

"Uh yeah, I sure do Tony," I said, not believing what I was saying, but my dick seemed to have taken over.

I positioned myself at the entrance to Blake's hole and took over from Tony after he had pulled his dick out.

"*Oh* yeah, fucking nice and tight Blake, I've wanted to fuck your ass for years," I heard myself saying and started pumping the poor guy harder and harder.

"*Oh yeah,* fuck me Jeff!" roared Blake and I could not believe what the fuck I was hearing.

My straight buddy wanted me to fuck him. I saw the red light on the camera in the wall, but I just couldn't stop myself. I kept fucking Blake in the ass over the couch. I slowly pulled out and rolled him over onto his back on the couch and re-entered him, hoisting his legs up, up, UP. Oh yeah, he felt so nice and tight and now I could see his face as I fucked him harder and harder.

To my further disbelief Blake was smiling up at me as I pounded his ass. Like Tony had done I pinched his nips and even toyed with his hard dick. I leaned down and kissed him as I fucked him. To my surprise he kissed me back. Oh yeah, I thought, I've been waiting for this for a long fucking time.

"Oh yeah Blake, take my fucking dick," I crooned down at the guy.

I had gotten so involved with Blake that I didn't realize what Tony was doing. He had taken up a position behind me and lubing my hole. Oh man, that felt so good as he played with my hole, fingered and moistened it with the lube as I fucked and fucked Blake, and then he entered me. Oh fuck, I'd never felt that before, being fucked while I was fucking someone else.

"*Oh man,* I'm going to cum soon!" I yelled out as much to myself as anyone else, but Blake was right there with me.

He started shooting his load the moment I did. Tony then started shooting just as I was finishing. Oh man that felt wild having him cum in me as I finished.

I collapsed on top of Blake, but gave him a long kiss and he kissed me back. Tony gave me a slap on the butt and said, "You both have fucking hot asses. And man, I got it all on tape."

With that he punched a few buttons and we saw the screen with all three of us on it, fucking. I started to panic. What if my co-workers saw something like this?

Tony saw the look of panic on both mine and Blake's faces…

"Relax," he said. "This is for my own private viewing, well, mostly just me."

Then he paused and said, "As long as you both keep coming over for Saturday football games, no problem." He grinned meanly and continued, "Next week's game is at two PM. I'll have a few more friends over, and there will be a pre-game tape show starring you guys, Blake and Jeff, so you'll need to be here at one. It'll be good for my friends to meet the stars of the tape they'll see." And with that said Tony grinned at me and Blake. We both looked scared as all hell, but neither of our boners had gone down. How in the hell was I going to survive the next week?

Tony then tossed our clothes to me and Blake and said, "Get dressed porn stars. You'll need to rest up for next week."

Blake and I quickly got dressed and left to go back to my apartment. We didn't say anything till we got there. Once I had closed and locked the door Blake turned to me and apologized for having made the bet. I told him, "I'm not sorry Blake. I finally got to fuck you."

He turned to me and started kissing me, saying, "That was hot Jeff, it's a shame it took this to make me realize I wanted you, but man what a predicament we're in now," in between planting kisses on me everywhere. I looked down and we were both still hard...

TELLING IT TO A MARINE
(EVERY WHICH WAY POSSIBLE)

My name is Clifton Davis. I'm a United States marine, and mighty damned proud of it let me tell you. I'm twenty-four years old, I have light brown hair, cut real high and tight ala marine style, brown hair, green eyes and I'm about five feet nine inches tall. When I was in New York last summer during Fleet Week two damned scoundrels and some of their mean buddies decided to play a twisted joke on me, I suppose it can be said it made their day and got them their jollies to have one upped on a United States marine of all people. Allow me please to tell you about it. I'm stationed in Georgia, my hometown, and my superior officer granted me a two week vacation leave, beginning with Fleet Week in New York City. Overjoyed, I told my superior officer how I had never been to New York and could not wait to get there. I had *never* seen the great city and was always so very curious about it. I hightailed it out of Georgia on a big old Greyhound bus and arrived in New York ten hours later. Most of the people on the bus were bushed after the long ride, but not me. I was so damned excited about being in the Big Apple that I could hardly contain myself. Neatly and sprucely dressed in my green dress marine uniform I checked into an inexpensive hotel on thirty-Third Street and Seventh Avenue and went out to begin sightseeing. I had my camera with me. What I failed to notice were the two scoundrels sitting in the lobby of the hotel that were looking at me most lustfully as I left the hotel.

I had a hearty breakfast in a small diner, took some pictures with some pretty girls who asked if I would pose with them, I blushed three different shades of red when one of the girls pecked me on the cheek after thanking me for taking pictures with them, and then went to see The Empire State Building, Rockefeller Center, and even had lunch at a classy restaurant in the theater area. Besides posing for pictures with pretty girls I took as many pictures as I could of everything with my camera. I purchased tickets for a Broadway show and sat in the balcony of the theater and watched Nathan Lane and a great cast perform a show called "A Funny Thing Happened On The Way To The Forum." Wonderful show! But by then it was late evening and feeling somewhat tired I decided to have a couple of beers before dinner and then calling it a night. I found a pretty big bar and grill about a block away from the hotel I was staying at and went in.

I found a vacant seat at the front bar and ordered an ice cold Budweiser. The bartender, a real friendly New Yorker dude placed the beer and a napkin in front of me. I thanked him and took a hearty marine sized swig of the beer.

"*AHHH!*" I exclaimed as I put the bottle down.

"Bet that tastes good huh Solider boy?" I heard a voice behind me ask.

"Huh?" I asked, turning quickly to see one of the scoundrels I've been mentioning.

He was pretty damned tall with black hair and real dark eyes. His friend, standing next to him was equally tall but with lighter hair and lighter eyes.

"Er – yeah, I sure do love beer," I replied. "But I'm not a soldier, I'm a marine."

"Sorry for the mistake," the first guy said apologetically. "I can't tell one uniform from the other. I'm Lamar, and this is my friend Jack."

I shook hands with both of them and introduced myself. They politely asked if they could join me and I said, "Yes." (Big mistake.) They sat down on the stools on the sides of me that had recently been vacated, putting me in the center of them.

"Hey Mike, get us some Buds here," Lamar called out to the bartender. "And give Clifton another beer as well, on us."

I thanked them kindly and asked, "You two know the bartender?"

"Sure we do Clifton ol' boy," Lamar said, giving me a hard clap on the shoulder.

The bartender placed three beers on the bar in front of us and gave Lamar a nasty look. Too bad I didn't ask about it, it might have saved me some real trouble. We all raised our beers and Lamar proposed a toast to the United States marines. We all drank heartily. Jack finally joined the conversation by asking where I was stationed and what I was doing in New York. I happily told them that I was on a two week vacation and enjoying Fleet Week as well. They looked at each other around me and smiled. Lamar placed a hand on my shoulder and said that if I wanted he and Jack would happily show me around New York. I thanked him but told him that I would rather see the Big Apple on my own and at my own pace.

"Suit yourself handsome," Lamar said and took another swig of his beer.

"I uh, do hope I didn't hurt your feelings there Sir," I said, looking at Lamar.

"Nah, not at all," Lamar replied, placing his fingers around my beige uniform necktie. "Your tie is a little crooked Soldier boy."

As Lamar straightened my tie for me I didn't see Jack slip a tiny pill into my beer.

"There you go," Lamar said, finishing with my tie.

I took a good gulp of my beer and told the two men that the next day I was planning on seeing The Statue of Liberty. They agreed that that was a great thing to do. After two more swigs from my beer I began to feel woozy.

"Man, I must really be getting tired," I said, leaning my head down. "I feel so dang-ed woozy all of a sudden."

Lamar unscrewed the top from my second beer and put it to my lips.

"Drink up Soldier boy," he insisted. "It's all the excitement in New York that's got you woozy."

I sipped the beer and slurred that I was a marine, not a soldier boy, correcting Lamar again.

"Sure you are," Jack said, placing a hand on the back of my buzz haircut-ed head. "Lamar, maybe we should help this handsome marine back to his hotel. If memory serves me correctly he's staying in room five nine eight at the Rogers.

"H–how do you know that?" I asked through slurred speech and blurred vision at that point.

Jack took my flap hat off my head, placed it atop his head and before I could object he and Lamar were holding one of my arms each.

"C'mon Soldier boy, we'll help you to your room," Lamar said.

"Th–thank you," I said sheepishly. "B–but I'm a marine…
not a soldier boy."

The two men half walked half carried me quickly to the
hotel. When we arrived there they hustled me quickly through the
lobby. No one was on duty at the front desk and no one was sitting
in the lobby either. And no one outside had wondered what the two
dudes were doing helping what seemed like a drunk marine, I'm
sure it was a usual sight after all in New York during Fleet Week.
They got me to the bank of elevators and Jack pressed the button.
When the elevator doors slid open we all stepped in. Lamar pressed
the button marked five and in my haze I could have sworn that the
two men were taking turns kissing me on the lips.

"Fucking beautiful marine he is…" I heard Lamar say from
far away.

When we got to my room Lamar fished the key out of my
uniform jacket pocket and opened the door. Jack picked me up
onto his huge shoulders and I heard Lamar say, "We're home," the
door closed and I passed out.

The Next Morning…

I woke up slowly and to my horror found myself tied to the
small single bed in my room by my wrists and ankles. *And damn,*
I was wearing just my white briefs and my black nylon calf length
dress socks. The bastards, they had stripped me of my uniform,
my pride and joy! As I opened my eyes I saw Lamar and Jack
sitting at the writing table in my hotel room. Like me they were
also wearing just their underwear. My uniform was on the floor
along with my flap hat and black patent leather lace-up shoes. The
two scoundrels were sipping coffee as they sat at the small table.

I noticed saliva stains on my briefs and bight marks on my chest. Damn, they'd been at me while I was unconscious!

"You fucking scoundrels!" I roared at them as I thrashed helplessly on the bed. "*Shit!*"

"Looks like our soldier boy is awake," Jack said happily and he and Lamar rose from their chairs and stepped over to me.

They each knelt on either side of the bed I was tied to.

"What is this shit?" I demanded.

"Just having some fun with you Soldier boy," Lamar replied, taking one of my nipples between his thumb and first finger. "Don't worry; no real harm will come to you."

"You two scoundrels are faggots!" I screamed in his face.

"You're so right Soldier boy, and we got you," Jack said to me as he reached into my danged briefs and pulled out my semi-hard dick along with my balls. "Got you easier than taking candy from a baby… as the saying goes…"

He held my meat and balls in his hand and looked at them adoringly.

"Jeez, this soldier boy has some monster sized dick Lamar," Jack said passionately.

"I'm a goddamned marine!" I roared. "Not a pussy soldier boy! Now you two untie me and get out of my damned room!"

But alas, they ignored me and Lamar leaned his head down and took one of my nipples into his mouth and began sucking, licking and nipping it while with his hand he pinched and squeezed my other nipple. Jack slurped my big dick into his mouth and began sucking it, licking it, and fucking kissing the tip of it.

"*OOOHHH shit*… you fucking perverts…" I moaned in anger and ecstasy at the same danged time. "*Ssshhhiiittt…*"

I watched with my head raised as they worked the fuck out of my nipples and dick. Jack even tongued my big marine sized balls a few times and sniffed hungrily at my briefs. I knew that it wouldn't be too long before I shot my load.

"*OHHH…*" I crooned.

Then, as Jack sucked me harder and harder I did indeed shoot a giant load of white marine spew into his mouth.

""*OHHH* yeah, fucking bastards, kidnap a poor marine so you can make him cum?" I garbled crazily.

My head bounced up and down on the bed as u watched the scoundrel swallowed my precious juices.

"Oh you bastard, swallowing my marine sized sacred load!" I grunted breathlessly.

As I then laid there catching my breath Lamar quickly stripped off his briefs, straddled me, and forced my still hard dick into his asshole.

"*OOOHHH shittt!*" I screeched as he began rocking up and down on my pole. "Not-not again so soon you sick fucker!"

I was in pain and ecstasy at the same time as Lamar literally forced me to fuck his ass and forced me toward a second gusher at the same danged time.

"*ARRRGHHH!*" I roared helplessly and breathlessly.

Jack was too busy licking my damned feet as Lamar rocked on my hard dick.

"Fucking pervert!" I yelled. "Look at you licking my smelly damned socks!"

But then, my words were cut short as I shot my second load of the morning… into Lamar's hole.

"*OHHH God* of Gods," I shouted in heat. "I'm creaming in your damned hole you bastard!"

Lamar jacked himself off and shit his own load onto my big muscular robust chest as Jack spewed his juices all over my black socked feet. When we were all spent Lamar licked his cum off my chest, sucking and slurping at my nipples at the same time and Jack greedily slurped his cum off my smelly day old socks.

"Damn Lamar," Jack said. "When we're done here I'm keeping these socks of his as a souvenir."

"No problem Jack my man, no problem," Lamar said as he packed my dick back into my briefs.

"Untie me now you two scoundrels!" I barked. "I want you two out of here so I can get on with my sightseeing!"

"HA, unfortunately the only sights you'll be seeing today Boy is this room," Lamar said, squatting down next to me and placing a hand on the top of my head. "You see, we're inviting some of our friends here to meet... and... eat you..."

I saw Jack picking up the phone and dialing.

"Shit... no!" I yelled at Lamar. "*Please, man,* no!"

Lamar reached under the bed, produced a spray can with no markings on it of its contents, and pointed it directly at my nose.

"See you later Soldier boy," Lamar said and sprayed the contents of the spray can in my face.

"*UHHH...*" I grunted, my head fell back and I was asleep just about instantly.

The Same Morning...

I came around a short while later and saw Lamar opening the door to my hotel room. He greeted two men as they came in. I heard him call them Rodney and Patrick. Jack noticed me coming around and brought it to the men's attention. They all came over to the bed and hovered menacingly over me.

"Damn, he's fucking beautiful, so *hot!*" Rodney stated as he pulled off his shirt.

Lamar told them how I had already shot two big loads and how delicious my tits and dick were.

"Not to mention his stinking marine socked feet," Jack added mockingly.

"Get those briefs of his down and let's see how many more shots we can squeeze and tease out of him," Rodney said anxiously.

"I want to fuck him!" Patrick piped up, looking at me leeringly. "Tell me Marine, do you have a virgin ass or did your buddies pop your cherry?"

"You fuck my ass and I swear *I will kill you!*" I roared up at the guy. "I've been trained to be a killing machine, see if I'm kidding you Pervert!"

"Now marine, you ain't in any position to be making threats like that!" Patrick laughed. "Rodney, let's get him off first. It'll hurt him more after he shoots a load or two when I fuck the tar out of him."

Lamar and Jack sat down at the writing table as Patrick and Rodney went to work on me.

The two men took turns sucking my dick up to a new hard-on and pinching my nipples at the same time, twisting them, really smarting the tar out of them.

"You bastards!" I bellowed up at them. "This is outright rape! And… and… oh shit, I'm going to fucking cum already!"

Patrick held my dick tightly in his hand as I shot my damned third load onto my stomach region.

"*Wow* wee!" Rodney hooted happily. "Just look at that marine squirt!"

"*OOOHHH…*" I moaned as my head bobbed up and down on the bed.

I was sweating like crazy then as Patrick and Rodney licked and lapped and ate my cum off my stomach, tickling me erotically, sending shivers and timbers through my muscular being.

"Fuckers, damned bastards," I whispered in a rage.

Then, to my dismay they stripped off their pants and untied my socked feet.

"Okay boy, are you ready?" Patrick asked me, holding my ankles in his hands.

"Please no, no…" I pleaded miserably.

"Rodney, jack this handsomer than handsome marine off as I fuck him!" Patrick ordered. "Boy, you are going to scream so loud they'll hear you back at your fucking base!"

"*No, oh God, no!*" I begged crazily as Patrick pushed my legs up and over my head, exposing my poor virgin asshole. He mounted the bed and his hard-on looked like it would never fit into my hole. Fuck, but it was gigantic! As the goddamned guy prepared to plow his dick into me Rodney closed a hand around my semi-hard dick.

"Oh God you bastards!" I reeled helplessly.

With no lube whatsoever on his dick or in my hole Patrick entered me a little at a time. The tip of his dick teased and tickled the front portion of my hole as Rodney slowly stroked my poor achin' dick. This would be my fourth shot when I came, not bad for a young studly marine huh dudes? Patrick's dick slowly found its way into me and I swear I could feel drops of pre-cum on the tip of it as he entered me a little more with each damned thrust. He, like Jack licked my danged socked feet as he held them tightly in his mangy hands by my ankles. I looked up at him beseechingly but then the inevitable happened… and he plunged his giant meat pole into my poor hole.

"*AYYYRRR!*" I screamed loudly and in a marine's pain as his dick hit home, opening my hole to new proportions.

"*Oh yeah, yeah!*" Patrick panted as he began to thrust wildly in and out and in and out of my hole.

"You lowlife fucking bastard!" I screamed in a high pitch.

I looked down at Rodney who was mercilessly stroking my dick, him hell-bent on getting another load of marine slop out of me.

"Let go man, damn that shit hurts!" I roared down at him as he stroked and choked my dick.

But then, to my total fucking disbelief, I shot a fourth load of my precious juices, this time onto my pubic bush.

"*Oh damn,* I'm cumming, cumming again you damned scoundrels!" I seethed through clenched teeth.

When I was done creaming for the fourth damned time Patrick's dick felt even bigger in my hole. I roared like a caged animal as he fucked me like a madman, fucked me like crazy, licking my danged stinking socked feet at the same time.

"*Oh* yeah, you hot fucking marine, you sexy jarhead, goddamned tight holed leatherneck," Patrick panted breathlessly. "I'm getting close now, of fucking *A*, yeah!"

When Patrick shot his load I felt his hot juices flood my hole.

"*OHHH* yeah, yeah, fucking *A*!" the guy screamed in a man's ecstasy as he shot and shot his load inside me, filling my hole with it.

When he was done, finally, his dick slipped out of my hole, he let my legs back down onto the bed, and he stood up next to the bed. Lamar and Jack dashed over to the bed and quickly retied my socked feet to the ends of the bed. Tears of rage, anger, and utter humiliation were rolling down my cheeks.

"Damn, that was good," Patrick said heartily.

Rodney leaned over my pubic hair bush and licked my cum off it, sucking at my pubic hair as well as he did. Then, the fucking guy jacked himself off onto my robust chest and licked that off me as well, slurping meanly at my nipples like a crazy man. I bucked and squirmed helplessly on the bed as the guy licked and sucked me like I was a lollipop. The other three men were amusing themselves by licking my danged smelly socked feet and even sucking my damned fingers. Then, Lamar, bastard that he is, sprayed the foul shit from the spray can into my face again, and I was out cold.

The Afternoon...

When I came around again Patrick and Rodney were gone and I was alone with Lamar and Jack. I was still tied to the bed and wearing just my briefs and socks. My poor dick was soft and hanging out of my briefs along with my balls. I smelled food... hotdogs. I guessed that my two captors had gone out for the hotdogs while I had been unconscious. Lamar came over to the bed with a hotdog in his hand.

"Hungry?" he asked me.

I nodded that I was and he lifted my head off the bed. He held the hotdog to my quivering lips and I took a small bight of it. I chewed it slowly.

"Damn you are beautiful," Lamar whispered as he fed me a second bight of the hotdog.

As I chewed the second bight Lamar licked a smear of mustard off the side of my lips. I was too exhausted to pull away from him. A few moments later I had finished eating the hotdog and Lamar let my head back down on the bed.

"Please man, no more..." I pleaded at him. "Please... let me go now..."

"Not so fast Soldier boy," Lamar said, wiping my lips with a napkin. "We still want more of you."

"Goddamn..." I muttered miserably.

Jack came over to the bed and squatted on the opposite side of Lamar. They each took one of my nipples into their mouths and began sucking them most earnestly. Within what seemed like scant minutes my dick was achingly hard again.

"Okay, that's just what we wanted," Lamar said. "Now, stop working his nipple and tie up his dick and balls.

"Wh–what?" I panted.

Doing as Lamar had ordered Jack produced a small length of rope and tied it tightly around where my dick meets my balls.

"Shit, that fucking guy is tying up damned dick and balls!" I shouted at Lamar. "What the hell am I in for now?"

In response I heard a knock at the door.

"That's Bob and Lenny," Lamar said to me, stroking my hair. "Soldier boy, you are in for a painful orgasm, number five that is."

Lamar pointed at my dick and balls as Jack ran to open the door.

"Shit…" I whispered helplessly

Bob and Lenny were two more of Lamar and Jack's sex crazy friends. They were both pretty muscular and both of them were very tall. They each had light brown hair and brown eyes. As soon as they were in the room Lamar showed me off to them and they quickly stripped off their clothes.

"And here we go again," I said to myself miserably as the two men leaned down over my trussed up dick and balls.

Bob gobbled my hard dick into his mouth as Lenny meanly tongued my balls… hard and painfully. I screamed in a marine's pain and agony but my cries went unheeded. If anything my cries seemed to spur the two dick and balls hungry dudes on all the more. I saw Jack squat down at my left foot and begin licking it. That fucking scoundrel just couldn't leave my damned socked feet alone!

"Thanks for tying and packaging his dick and balls," Bob said to Lamar in between sucking me off. "I love seeing a guy with his privates in this way. It makes him scream even more when he gushes."

And sure enough I screamed mighty danged loud when Bob managed to force the fifth gusher out of me, suctioning my cock hard and swallowing the small amount of marine jazz that erupted out of my piss hole…

Bob and Lenny left shortly afterward. They didn't stay to get themselves off. I supposed that they just wanted the glory of seeing a trussed up captive marine shoot his load. I laid there totally breathless and exhausted. Lamar once more sprayed the stinking canned chloroform in my face, putting me back to sleep for a while…

That Night…

When I woke up much later I saw that it had gotten dark outside. I was no longer tied to the bed and my danged socks were gone from my feet. Lamar and Jack were gone also. I bolted off the bed, wearing just my briefs and dashed to the bathroom where I pissed like crazy… fuck, I pissed like a real marine buds. After using the bathroom I took a long hot shower and ordered dinner sent up to my room. I ate alone thinking what an interesting trip New York had turned out to be.

A Year Later…

I never saw Lamar or Jack or any of their friends after that encounter in New York. I've tried to find them through ads I've placed in gay publications, Facebook, MySpace and all other social media networks you can mention, but I've received no responses whatsoever. So Lamar, Jack, if you guys happen to read this please do get in touch with me. I'm one fucking horny marine who has learned the joys of what you taught me. I'm ready for more you scoundrels!

RICK THE LAUNDRY GUY WATCHES THE SECOND ENCOUNTER BETWEEN ALEX AND JASON

I work as the laundry collector for the Boston Red Sox baseball team. I was there that day. I saw everything and I'm not just talking about the clash they had on the field. I'm talking about what transpired later on, after the game, in the Red Sox locker room of all places. My hero Jason kicked that guy Alex's ass on the field, but I suppose that Alex's Latin blood mixed with a Latin temper and mixed with his Latin machismo was not able to let it go. The look on his face as he had walked off the field after getting his ass whipped by my hero Jason was one of total humiliation. I'm sure you know what I'm talking about if you saw the game and if you saw the pictures in all the newspapers the next day. Alex was totally pissed off and humiliated at the same time. What a combination of emotions for a poor macho guy to suffer let me tell you. As I said I was there that day and I saw everything. And man, what I saw happen after the game, in that locker room, will *never* make the news or newspapers.

The game ended late in the afternoon and all the other players for the Boston Red Sox had already showered and gotten changed into street clothes and were on their way home to wives, girlfriends or perhaps significant others; all of them that is except for Jason. Because of what had transpired on the field he had been besieged by reporters for commentary concerning the violent eruption between him and Alex on the field. He said things how he hadn't wanted it to happen but the guy had driven him to it. In the privacy of the locker room after the reporters had left certain teammates said how they were glad that Jason had kicked the handsome Alex's ass, and right there for all the world to see. One player commented how the look of anger mixed with defeat in Alex's eyes was so fucking classic to see. The guy was totally humiliated. And being that he had brought it on made most of the team agree that he had deserved to get his pretty ass kicked. While the players talked about the incident, how it would be in all the papers the next day and on the news and on the internet I made my way around the locker room collecting dirty uniforms, rancid sweat and piss stained underwear, stinky jockstraps and smelly sweat socks, all red sweat socks actually, the team's signature socks and deposited all the dirty laundry in my wheel-away cart.

By the time I was nearly done collecting all the dirty laundry only Jason was left in the locker room. He hadn't showered yet and when I approached him he was sitting on the bench in front of his open locker clad in just his moist looking jockstrap and high red signature sweat socks.

"Hey there Jason," I said as I picked up his dirty uniform from the floor and put it in my cart, taking in his sweaty manly scent as I leaned down near his feet where his uniform was strewn on the floor in front of his locker.

"Hey Rick, how are you man?" Jason asked, looking at me and smiling. "Sorry to have taken so long in getting undressed man. But with the reporters and all…"

"I understand Sir," I said, drinking in the sight of his toes wiggling under his high red socks as he sat there looking up at me.

It was amazing to me how those high red socks that he was wearing had just seen his feet through nine grueling innings, had seen him kick Alex's pretty ass on the field and they were still nice and snug around his tree-trunk like legs, all the way up to just under his knees. I supposed that the guy made sure he had snug socks, didn't want to have anyone see them falling down in case of photo opportunities. I've always admired the baseball players who choose to favor that style of high socks that has become so fashionable nowadays.

"I mean, of all the fucked up things huh? Me, getting involved in a goddamned exchange of fisticuffs on the field with a player from an opposing team," Jason said. "I mean, fuck, that's not me you know? I mean, like any other guy I can get angry if someone pushes my buttons or twists my nuts the wrong way, but fuck; I'm not usually prone to violent outbursts like that. I guess that fucking guy really pissed me off huh?"

"Well, obviously that guy really pushed your buttons the wrong way," I said, sounding sympathetic.

"Yeah, he sure as hell did, that goddamned pretty boy, how they all make such a big deal over him huh?" Jason said angrily and curled one of his big hands into a fist, punching his other open hand with it. "Ha, there's that temper of mine again Rick! I know most times I can control my temper but today I just lost it man! That team wanted him because he's eye candy! I mean, okay, he's a good baseball player but he's eye candy first, fucking pretty boy!

FUCK, but that guy pissed me off, cursing at me on the field like that! Who the fuck did he think he was huh?"

"Yeah, but you sure as hell kicked his sorry ass," I laughed as Jason got to his feet and took a bar of soap and a washcloth from the top shelf of his locker and placed them on the bench he had been sitting on.

"I sure as fuck did, didn't I Rick?" Jason said with a sneer on his ruggedly handsome face, his dark hair all sweaty and askew, his goatee making that sneer look all the more sinister. "Fuck man, I really showed that narcissistic bastard who was the boss. Now you know what would be really great if it were to happen Rick?"

"What's that Jason sir?" I asked as he handed me his sweaty tee shirt from his locker and I deposited it in my laundry cart.

"If we could get in the playoffs, win it and then head on to win the World Series," Jason said, with a grin now on his ruggedly handsome face and scratching his sweaty balls in his jockstrap at the same time. "Man, if that shit would happen we would be sitting pretty Rick. The fucking so called curse would be broken..."

"It sure would Jason Sir, it sure would," I said, stealing a glance downward as the hunky guy scratched his nuts and I saw that he was sporting a semi erection in his jockstrap.

"Although I don't believe in any goddamned curses you know?" the muscular and hairy chested baseball player said to me in the form of a question. "I think it's just been good rotten luck that has caused that team to best us all these years..."

"Maybe that's why you really reeled into Alex out there, all that pent-up frustration," I suggested.

"Yeah, or maybe I just wanted to teach the pretty boy a real lesson," Jason laughed and so did I.

"Well, I'm just about done collecting all the dirty uniforms and accessories," I said. "Would you want me to take your jockstrap and socks?"

"Huh? Oh yeah sure thing Rick," Jason said and balanced himself on one foot each time he slid his high red socks off feet and then took off his jockstrap as well.

I could not help but take in the sight of his long and as pointed out already, semi hard manhood as it hung all sweaty and randy between his tree trunk like legs, his big hairy nut sac hanging real low under them, his balls looking like they were the size of golf balls, all juicy and succulent in that silky and hairy sac of his.

"Here you go buddy," Jason said and handed me his moist red socks and equally moist jockstrap. "I'm going to hit the showers now and then be on my way."

"Sounds good to me Sir," I said, holding his socks all bunched up in my hand real tight after having dropped his jockstrap into my cart. "I may still be here when you're done. I have to make one last round around the locker room to be sure I don't leave anything behind."

"Okay cool, I'll be out of here real soon, I have a formal family thing to go to when I get dressed," he said, pointing at his locker where I saw a dark blue suit hanging. "Got to get myself all prettied and into a monkey suit…"

Again we both laughed and then I watched as the guy picked up his bar of soap, his washcloth, a fresh pair of white briefs and a pair of navy blue OTC nylon dress socks and walked to the shower area… My heart thudded in my chest at the sight of those hairy well-toned ass globes of his as he walked naked away from me, a cocky and confident stride in his step as he walked… His ass globes were the shapes of two coconuts… I could almost imagine the stink that must have been emanating from between Jason's hairy ass globes at that moment. What I would not have given to bask with my face pressed between his globes and just eat the raunchiness that had collected there during the game in the grueling hot sun… But alas, all I could do was take a hearty sniff of the musty manly scented locker room air and go about finishing up my tasks.

In the shower area Jason put his socks and underpants down on a shelf, helped himself to a towel, hung the towel on a hook outside the shower stall he chose and then stepped into the warm spray of water with his bar of soap and washcloth...

While Jason showered I collected whatever last remnants of clothing were still strewn about the locker room. I had Jason's red socks hanging out of the back pocket of my work pants. When I found an area where no one would see me (just in case someone was still in the locker room) I took Jason's socks from my pocket and with my hands trembling did what I had wanted to do for the longest time. I bunched Jason's red socks up in one hand and held the toes section of them to my nose and mouth. They smelled of a mixture of cleats leather, man sweat and real foot stink. I stuck out my tongue and licked at the fronts of them a few times and inhaled their funky odor.

"Jason," I whispered, imagining the tough guy wearing these very socks just a short time ago out on the baseball field when he had kicked that guy's ass, and he had it coming to let me tell you.

In all the time that I had been the laundry collector for this team I never once got to sniff Jason's socks. When I collect laundry most times the team is still there and if any of them were to catch me sniffing their dirty sweaty socks or their underwear or their jockstraps I would most likely be thrown out on my ear. But today, because of a fight on the field, because Jason was delayed in the locker room and I suppose because of good karma I got really lucky...

I again held Jason's randy socks to my nose and mouth and inhaled. I thought of him wearing these socks all those hours out on the field, how his feet had sweated in them while encased in his cleats, how he had kicked Alex's ass while wearing them. They would become my lucky socks. Someday Jason would be inducted into the baseball hall of fame and I would have these socks of his... I inhaled them again and the scent of Jason's sweaty feet filled my nostrils and my cock became rock hard in my workpants...

When I heard the shower water turned off a little while later I quickly stashed Jason's socks in my deep pockets and went around on my last round of collecting dirty laundry in the locker room. It was around that time that Jason finished up in the shower and while I was collecting the last of the dirty laundry that Alex made his way into the locker room and all hell broke loose again between the two rival baseball players...

When Jason finished showering he dried off, stepped out of the shower and put on his navy blue OTC nylon dress socks and his white briefs. And fuck, the way those ass globes of his looked in those tight white briefs of his, man, *fucking awesome!* Standing in front of a mirror he shaved and groomed his goatee a bit and slicked his black silky hair back with some hair gel. For some reason the guy looked real suave and real vulnerable standing there shaving while wearing just his fresh briefs and thin navy blue dress socks. He tossed his towel in a cart that is always in the shower area and headed back to his locker to get into his suit for whatever family gathering he was headed to that evening. I was a few rows away from Jason's locker but I heard it clearly when his rugged voice boomed out the words, "What the fuck are you doing here Alex? This isn't your goddamned team's locker room!"

My ears perked up at the sounds of the two rival baseball player's voices as they again argued...

Alex had waited purposely it seemed for the rest of the team members to exit the locker room, knowing somehow (or perhaps hoping) that Jason would be the last one there and at the same time be left alone, easy pickings, so Alex thought. Alex obviously wanted revenge on Jason for what had happened earlier out on the field and he figured that the best place to get it would be right on Jason's turf, right in the team's locker room of all places. Alex hadn't even changed out of his team uniform. Fuck, he hadn't even showered or anything. It was as if all he had on his mind was revenge. As the two handsome men began arguing I silently made my way to a spot where I could watch the exchange between them...

"Who the hell even let you in here man?" Jason was saying angrily, standing wearing just his navy blue OTC nylon dress socks and white briefs, standing in front of his open locker, almost nose to nose with Alex, just as they had been earlier on the field. "Fuck, when something stinks as bad as you, both as a baseball player and as a guy there should be rules about just letting you into another team's locker room! Shit, your stink will pollute this place man!"

As Jason ranted the muscles in his huge arms seemed to flex involuntarily...

"I let myself in man; you owe me and my teammates a goddamned apology!" Alex seethed, holding up a long finger, wagging it in Jason's face practically. "And fuck your insults man!"

Alex had the same look on his face at that moment that he had had when he walked off the field earlier as a beaten man...

"Apology for what you asshole?" Jason ranted back at his opponent. "You overreacted, you made a scene in front of millions of people, you cursed me out on the field and you got your sorry ass kicked for it!"

"Like hell I did man, but like I said you owe me and my team an apology, and I'll get an apology for you calling me an asshole just now as well," Alex said, hefting one foot up and resting it on the bench in front of Jason's locker, looking at him real smugly.

"Look Alex, I really don't feel like arguing with you while I'm wearing just my goddamned under shorts and dress socks here, you know?" Jason said, holding Alex's stare with his eyes, not letting the guy see that he was curling one hand into a big and meaty fist. "I'm feeling all sexy and real vulnerable here man and…"

But before Jason finished his sentence he raised his fist in what seemed like lightning speed and brought it crashing against the very handsome Alex's face, clocking him good and hard…

"*HOOOFFFF!*" Alex grunted, his foot that had been up on the bench slid off as he stumbled and tumbled backward, the back of his head hitting the locker next to Jason's. "*UUHHHNNNFFF!* Shit…"

"Bet you came here looking for some kind of revenge huh buddy boy?" Jason asked and grabbed two handfuls of Alex's team uniform shirt, hefting him meanly away from the locker he had just rammed against so involuntarily. "But I kind of get the feeling that you're going to get more of the same of what I gave you out on the field, and maybe worse this time… seeing as it's just you and me here, no one to break us up this time!"

That said Jason clenched his teeth, summoned as much strength as possible and yanked Alex off his sneaker feet by his uniform shirt, Jason's huge biceps straining with his effort. Alex's feet left the floor, he found himself sailing over the bench between the rows of lockers and Jason slammed him this time against a locker on the opposite side of his…

The sound of Alex's muscular back hitting the locker was loud and metallic…

"*UHHHNNFFF!*" Alex gasped, having been taken totally by surprise.

"So much for revenge huh asshole?" Jason asked the guy as he slid to the floor in front of the locker, his knees bent up as he slid downward.

"*Ahhh*, shit," Alex mumbled a look of misery etched on that handsome face of his.

It was obvious to me that Alex's head was spinning and there wasn't much he was going to be able to do as Jason dished it out on him a second time that day…

"So what were you expecting man that I was going to apologize to you for what you caused?" Jason asked Alex, reached down and grabbed a handful of the guys' sweaty and mussed hair, yanking upwards meanly.

"*OWWWRRR! You fucker!*" Alex reeled and as he was lifted upwards by his hair I could tell that he came sailing out of that stupor he had been knocked into right quickly, but only for the moment, as I (and he) were about to find out.

Through the pain he was being dealt Alex kicked his sneaker feet outwards, trying to gain some balance, trying to find a way to overturn this awful turn of events that had befallen him. Unfortunately, Jason saw what Alex was up to and made short work of him by kicking his sneaker feet out from under him with one long socked foot.

"*UUHHHNNFFF!*" Alex said yet again as he landed this time on his sexy ass, Jason letting go of his hair. "I–I fucking demand that you apologize for what you did to me out on the field and for what you just did to me here…"

A look of total disbelief came over Jason's handsome face as Alex was now on his hands and knees, his sexy round ass up in the air as he tried again to gain his feet.

"And I expect you to apologize publicly," Alex went on, slowly getting himself up off the floor, his back still to his opponent. "That way you'll feel the same humiliation I felt out there…"

"You really are some piece of work buddy boy, and not to mention a real fucking glutton for punishment," Jason laughed sadistically, stepped quickly behind Alex, reached down and grabbed the back of the guy's belt with two hands. "What about the humiliation you're feeling in here now, how about that Alex?"

Again, summoning all his strength Jason clenched his teeth and hoisted his opponent like he was a piece of luggage.

"*HOOOFFF*, h–hey, *hey!*" Alex howled as he was lifted by the seat of his pants. "*Holy fucking fuck!*"

The guy swung his arms out uselessly in front of himself as Jason lifted him a tad higher, the muscles in his huge biceps flexing involuntarily and erotically as he carted the heavy load of Alex. I sniffed Jason's red sweat socks and watched the spectacle as it unfolded in front of me…

"*Put me the fuck down!*" Alex bellowed when he saw that his head was aimed at a locker…

"What's the matter buddy boy? When you got your ass kicked out on the field you were pissed off, why shouldn't you be now too while you get your ass kicked again huh?" Jason teased Alex meanly.

"You fucking fucker, you fucking fucked up guy!" Alex crowed miserably as he swung his arms out in front of himself. "I didn't plan on getting my ass kicked again! Fucking fucks Fucker; I planned on getting an apology from you! Fucking totally fuck, I thought you would be a goddamned gentleman about it, but fuck, I guess I was wrong huh?"

"That's just one too many fucking fucks Alex buddy," Jason quipped and gripped Alex's belt tighter.

He hefted his load higher and then Alex found himself propelled forward and the front of his forehead connected meanly with a locker. The sound was another *CLANG*…

"*OWWW*, shit, d–dirty fighter," Alex whimpered as he slid down against the locker again…

I then watched as Jason hauled the guy to his feet by the back of his belt, whirled him around and with one hand grabbed a goodly amount of Alex's team uniform shirt. Alex was winded

and disoriented and he wobbled stupidly in Jason's grasp, his head
bobbing up and down.

"Got a good one for you now buddy boy, and right in the
kisser too," Jason chuckled, sounding totally sadistic.

"*Wha...*" was all Alex could say as Jason then raised an
open palmed hand.

Jason reached back, *far back*, and with mighty force swung
his arm forward, let go of Alex's uniform shirt and *rapped* Alex
hard across the face.

"*YUHHH!*" Alex reeled, spun once on his cleated feet,
wobbled about miserably and landed facedown over the bench
between the rows of lockers, his ass in the air. "*AYYY...*"

Looking down at his again beaten opponent as he lay there
whimpering miserably Jason chuckled sadistically once more,
reached down, grabbed the back of Alex's belt and hauled the
poor guy to his feet again... Jason walked him toward the shower
area, Alex shuffling and stumbling along, in a definite daze at that
point...

"Y–you said you felt real vulnerable in your dress socks
and briefs," Alex said softly, five fingermarks adorning his cheek
where Jason had just so meanly backhanded him.

"Yeah, I did didn't I?" Jason responded sarcastically.
"Looks like high socks rule after all huh buddy boy? You should
try wearin' them some time... Now what do you say we give you a
shower huh asshole? You really could use one, seeing as you stink,
both on the field and as a fighter!"

"*F–fuck* you man," Alex grunted as he was pushed meanly
to the shower area, Jason holding him by the back of his belt and
one arm twisted painfully behind him.

"*Hey*, naw man, don't shower me with my goddamned
uniform still on me!" Alex ranted as Jason hauled him into the
same shower stall he had just used a short while ago. "*UFFFFF!*"

Alex hit the wall bodily, his crotch ramming into the faucets...

"*OHHH* jeez man," Alex panted, the breath again knocked out of him. "Holy fucking fucks..."

"We'll start off nice and cold huh bud?" Jason asked, gave the cold water faucet a twist and quickly stepped out of the stall.

"*ARRRHHH Gods!*" Alex screamed as he was doused with the icy cold water.

He stood with his palms against the tiled wall looking upwards into the cold spray; I suppose hoping that the cold water would clear his head somehow... He then lowered his hands, groping around in his daze for the water faucet to get it turned off and stop the infernal chill he was being dealt as the water pelted him. Jason quickly reached into the stall, grabbed Alex's hand as it groped for the faucet and slammed it against the tile wall.

"*ARRRHHH!*" Alex cried out. "Careful with my hands you bastard, I need 'em in good shape for the next game!"

Then I heard Jason say, "Now for a nice hot shower buddy boy," and the cold water was turned off and then Alex was pelted with hot steaming water...

"*AYYY* you b–bastard, you're soaking my goddamned uniform here!" Alex shrieked amid clouds of heated water.

"Best to get it off then huh bud?" Jason asked snidely and again reached into the shower stall.

He grabbed his dazed baseball opponent by his soaked hair and pushed his head forward. Poor Alex's forehead took another blow as it connected meanly with the tile wall.

"*UHHH!*" he gasped and slid down the wall in the shower stall.

"Didn't hurt your hands that time buddy boy, just your stupid pretty head," Jason laughed meanly.

Smiling meanly and totally sadistically Jason reached down and began unlacing Alex's cleats...

A short while later I heard the shower water turned off and watched, peeking from behind the row of lockers as Jason brought Alex out of the shower area. I was totally astounded by what I saw... Alex had been stripped of his baseball uniform down to his navy blue calf length sweat socks. Jason was holding the guy tight by his muscular upper arms yanked behind him as he led him dripping wet and still dazed out of the shower area... I wondered how Alex had felt being stripped of his uniform by the man who had kicked his sweet ass two times now in one day... and not to mention the fact that Jason was his baseball playing opponent. Alex had a bruise forming on his face and a lump was already starting to show on his forehead. He looked dazed and like he was in pain as he trudged along as Jason pushed him forward on his wet socked feet. Alex's feet made squishy noises against the tile floor as he was forced to plod along. Alex's muscular chest was jutted out and his nipples were totally erect looking. I could not help but notice the way the handsome baseball player's nipples were sticking up like two pink pencil erasers. A lot of guys have their nipples get like that while showering, or when they're really worked up sexually, or when they've just been thrown a beating, or all of the above. And not to mention that Alex's stalk was swinging semi hard in the wind and his hairy nuts were hanging and crashing against his thighs as he was unceremoniously led from the shower area...

"The laundry guy just left a while ago Alex my buddy," Jason said through clenched teeth, seeming to be taking in the sight of Alex's sexy ass as he walked him back to his locker area. "We got the whole stinking locker room all to ourselves..."

"L–leggo of me man," Alex seethed, struggling in Jason's tight grasp, heaving himself to his socked toes, doing anything he could to get free. "I'll teach you to rough me up and strip me like you did!"

"Now, now buddy boy, all that'll get you is more of this," Jason said as they approached his locker.

He heaved Alex upwards and then literally flung the guy toward his open locker...

"*ARRRHHH*!" Alex yelled as he landed with the front part of his well-toned body wedged comically inside Jason's locker.

He grabbed the sides of the locker to steady himself and moaned and groaned miserably over all of this.

I nearly blanched when Jason grabbed the cheeks of Alex's sweet ass to pry the guy out of his locker... Alex came out wobbly and sexy, his teeth clenched as Jason squeezed his ass cheeks like he was squeezing the goddamned Charmin.

"Okay buddy boy, now I have a real treat in store for you here," Jason said and kicked Alex's socked feet out from under him.

Alex toppled stupidly, swung his arms uselessly and landed on his stomach on the bench between the rows of lockers...

"*UUUHHHFFF*! *You* fucker," Alex snuffled.

"I always knew that I would find a use for this box of tricks," Jason said, taking a medium-sized cardboard box out of his locker.

"Wh–what?" Alex asked as he lay on his stomach on the bench, his muscular arms dangling at his sides, his upturned ass a real pretty picture.

Jason took the lid off the box and I nearly lost my piss when I saw the items that were in it. Alex was in for a hell of a time that day let me tell you... Standing there hidden I again raised my hero's red sweat socks to my nose and mouth and inhaled deeply...

"*Oh gawd*, wh–what are you doin' to me here?" Alex grunted angrily as he finally came around a short while later.

The pretty boy baseball player found himself still lying on the long bench at Jason's locker area, naked except for his navy blue sweat socks, obviously feeling totally humiliated. To add to his utter humiliation though Alex now found that his wrists had been roped together under the bench he was sprawled on, on his stomach. When he moved to stand up from the bench all he succeeded in doing was to raise his sexy ass upwards.

"H–holy fucking fucks man! You tied me up?" Alex squawked, his socked feet flat on the floor, his ass up in the air, his juicy looking cock and hairy sweaty balls dangling and swinging between his muscular tree trunk like legs and his hands bound in front of him under the bench, what a sight. "Fucker man, you tied me up, fucker you are Jason, what's the point of all this?"

"You tell me buddy boy," Jason laughed meanly, watching the spectacle of Alex struggling stupidly in front of him. "You're the one who came bounding in here like some half-cocked asshole! *HAR*, and now the bounder is bound up, *gotcha* good me buddy boy."

Alex struggled miserably to get his hands untied but his efforts were for naught, seeing as Jason had used mounds of rope on him and tied him real tight at that.

"Now you and I are going to have some real fun," Jason said, leaning down and giving Alex's ass cheeks a good hard resounding open handed swat.

"*OWWW! Gawd! Dirty fighter!*" Alex screamed, more in humiliation than in pain. "Got to tie a guy up to work him over? What kind of shit is that man?"

Thinking he could use it as a way to get free Alex heaved himself to his socked feet, clenched his teeth and scurried forward, moving almost like a spider. Unfortunately for the pretty baseball player the support beam at the end of, and under the bench stopped him in his socked tracks.

"Shit, shit, triple shit!" Alex blubbered.

"Were you planning on going somewhere buddy boy?" Jason asked Alex snidely, sitting down at the other end of the bench, his box of tricks at his side, the contents of which Alex had still not seen or taken notice of. "Come on back here cutey pie…"

As Jason spoke he made a "come here" gesture with his index finger, poor Alex looking back at him with his ass up in the air, his hairy and mangy hole exposed because of the position he was in, his cock and balls dangling between his thighs, and him looking back with a look of anger mixed with trepidation on his handsome face.

"Fucking untie me Jason, this isn't funny!" Alex crowed as he moved back toward his opponent ass first, not having much choice in the matter obviously.

"No, it's not funny yet buddy, but it's about to start getting funny, actually man, it's about to start getting hilarious," Jason snickered, watching with sadistic glee as Alex's gaping and open hole approached him.

When Alex was back in front of Jason's locker Jason sat down with his back to the guy, Alex's feet right where he could grab them very easily, and grab one of them he did buds, starting with the right one, just in case you need to know precisely…

"H–hey, what are you up to man?" Alex cried out as Jason hooked his socked foot up by the ankle and held it tight in one hand, the fingers of his other hand aimed for the bottom of it.

Alex found himself lying prone on his stomach on the bench as Jason held his captive foot real tight, pulling it close to his lap in his grip.

"Let go of my goddamned foot Jason!" Alex prattled. "I didn't make mention of this before but my teammates know that I came here looking for you! When I don't show up back at our locker room real soon they'll come looking for me! And fuck man, they will get you for this!"

"Yeah, but the real question is, will they get you? And if you think I believe that I'll bet you have a bridge I can buy," Jason laughed and proceeded to press his fingertips against the bottom of Alex's right foot. "Now tell me buddy boy, are you a ticklish dude?"

"T–ticklish? Me? Ticklish? What the fucking fuck do you mean by that Jason?" Alex asked, the look on his face now one of almost mortal fear.

"I suppose that if you're not going to answer me I'll just have to find out for myself huh?" Jason asked and started scribbling and scrabbling his fingertips up and down the bottom of Alex's socked foot that he had in hand.

"*AAAAAYYY Ha, ha, ha, ha, ha, ha, ha, ha, ha, ha, ha, ha! Holy fucking shit,* s–stop that Jason!" Alex screamed in laughter. "STOP that this instant!"

Alex cowed on the bench and in between laughing he tried desperately to get his hands untied…

"Oh man, check this out, the prettiest baseball player in the world, having his smelly feet tickled," Jason quipped.

Then, Jason quickly held Alex's right foot between his steely-like thighs, reached down, grabbed Alex's other foot, and now he had both of Alex's socked feet at his disposal for whatever he planned to do with them, namely, tickle them…

He drummed his fingertips up and down and up and down and across and back and forth on the bottoms of both of Alex's socked feet as he held them trapped between his strong thighs.

"*AAAAAARRRHHH Ha, ha, ha, ha, ha, ha, ha, ha, ha, ha, ha, OHHHRRR gawd man!*" Alex railed helplessly, looking forward and laughing, tears filling his beautiful eyes. "I–I haven't been tickle tortured since me and my siblings were kids! *HAR, HAR, HAR, HAR, HAR, HAR, HAR!*"

"Then I would say that it's safe to assume that you were due for it buddy boy," Jason laughed meanly and lifted both of Alex's feet in his hands. "Long overdue more than likely I would say…"

He yanked Alex's feet forward till they were wrapped around his body up to Alex's thighs as he sat there on the bench facing away from him. My cock grew harder as I saw that Alex was wiggling his toes under his sweat socks and I saw that Jason was doing the same thing under his OTC navy blue dress socks. Jason moved fast to push Alex's feet together in front of him at the chest and hold them fast in one big hand by the ankles. Poor Alex hadn't stopped laughing long enough to feel a semblance of relief before Jason began again in earnest tickling the bottoms of his size twelve's… This time Jason used the fingers of one hand, alternating back and forth between Alex's feet, giving them each the tickle time that they deserved. I also saw from the look on Jason's face that he was really digging his fingers into Alex's socked soles, not being the least bit stingy when it came to tickle torturing the fucking guy.

"*AAAAAYYY!* I cannot fucking believe that you're tickling my feet man, *ha, ha, ha, ha, ha, ha, ha, ha, ha, ha, ha, ha, ha!*" Alex sputtered, spittle flying from his mouth. "What a way to torture a poor guy, *ha, ha, ha, ha, ha, ha, ha, ha, ha, ha, HAR, HAR, HAR!*"

By now, Alex's tied hands were pressed flat against the floor as he lay on the bench, his socked feet held tightly and captive by the man who had become his arch enemy. Alex's cock was showing between his thighs and under his ass crack as he lay on that bench, totally at Jason's mercy…

"You know Alex, a lot of guys out there tend to think that tickling a guy isn't really torture," Jason laughed and strummed his fingertips along Alex's sexy arches. "But after this I'm sure you'll be able to tell all of them otherwise huh?"

Jason smiled from ear to ear, gave the bottoms of Alex's feet a playful swat each and lifted them a tad higher, closer to his face...

"*Ha, ha, ha, ha, ha, ha, ha, ha, ha, ha, ha, ha, ha, ha* s–stop, Jason, please stop!" Alex cackled. "I really am sooo fucking ticklish man!"

"Yes, I can see and hear that," Jason said agreeably and then pressed his nose against the bottom of one of Alex's sweat socked feet.

"*PWHAHHH* man, your fucking feet really stink Alex, just like you do!" Jason said, half disgustedly and half snidely, grinning while he said it.

"Who the fucking fuck told you to sniff my goddamned feet you bastard?" Alex cawed loudly in between bursts of laughter. "*Ha, ha, ha, ha, ha, ha, ha, ha, ha, ha, ha, ha, ha, ohhh gawd*, man, stop tickling me!"

"Stop? But Alex I'm just getting started here, and we haven't even gotten to my box of tricks yet," Jason said, sounding disappointed.

Jason grinned maniacally and again strummed his fingertips up and down the bottoms of poor Alex's socked feet.

"Your box of tricks?" Alex laughed. "*Ha, ha, ha, ha, ha, ha, ha,* what the fuck man, you been planning this or something?"

"Not really buddy boy, but one never knows when one will get to live out ones evil fantasies," Jason laughed and then let go of Alex's socked feet.

Alex's feet landed in Jason's lap, lying at their sides.

"Untie me and let me the fuck out of here man!" Alex yelled as Jason started pulling at Alex's socks, getting them slowly off his feet.

"Oh, first you come bounding in here after me like a bat out of hell and then when the tables turn on you, you want to leave?"

Jason asked his opponent, peeling Alex's socks from his feet as he spoke. "Sorry bud, but you're not leaving here till I'm done doing to you what I have in mind and until you've experienced my box of tricks…"

"Hey, what the fuck are you doing now man, taking my socks off my goddamned feet?" Alex hollered angrily through clenched teeth. "Fucking fuck man, those socks were the last shred of dignity you left me with Jason! Now you got me completely fucking naked here!"

"Keep bitching and moaning like that and I'll shove these stinking socks of yours in your mouth Alex me buddy," Jason laughed, dropped Alex's socks on the floor and reached into his box of tricks.

I could not help but notice that Jason was sporting an enormous and very plump erection in his briefs while his baseball opponent's now bare feet lay in his lap.

"Now, it's time for a good lesson in oral hygiene buddy boy," Jason said and held up an electric toothbrush.

"Oral hygiene?" Alex barked miserably, lifting his head and trying to crane it around to see what the hell Jason was up to.

The sound of the electric toothbrush coming to whirring life filled the locker area where Jason had his opponent trapped…

"H–hey, what the fuck is that sound Jason?" Alex asked, sounding terrified all of a sudden.

"Like I said buddy boy, it's time for a lesson in oral hygiene," Jason said and lowered the whirling bristles towards Alex's bare feet.

"Oral hygiene is for the teeth Jason and I am not in the mood for… *Ha, ha, ha, ha, ha, ha, ha, ha, ha, ha!*" Alex suddenly found himself filling the locker room with the sound of his raucous laughter. "H–holy fucking *shit*, what is that man? *Ha, ha, ha, ha, ha, ha, ha, ha, ha, ha, ha!*"

"It's an electric toothbrush buddy, and it's revved up to high speed, just for you," Jason laughed and rotated the whirling bristles over and over the bottoms of Alex's feet, his arches, and his heels.

"*Y–you fucker, Jason!*" Alex screamed helplessly, his toes wigging involuntarily as his poor feet were tickled and tickled. "*HAR, HAR, HAR, HAR, HAR, HAR, HAR!*"

"Ah, the sound of a man in the throes of laughter is music to my ears buddy boy," Jason said and held Alex's feet tighter as he tickled them alternately with the electric toothbrush. "And I have to admit that I always had a dream of being a dentist. But I found that if I became a professional baseball player instead I would make more money."

"*Ha, ha, ha, ha, ha, ha, ha, ha, ha, ha, ha, ha,* nice dream buddy boy!" Alex screamed crazily. "But brushing my feet is not what the dentist does, holy fucking shit! *HAR, har, har, har, har, har, har, har!*"

"All I can say is that you'd better hope that I don't decide to brush your teeth with this brush when I'm done ticking your smelly feet with it," Jason said.

"An–and when will that be you bastard? *HA, ha, ha, ha, ha, ha, ha, ha, ha, ha, ha, ha, ha,* wh–when are you going to stop tickling my goddamned feet?" Alex asked desperately.

"Ah, now that's a very good question Alex, a very good question indeed," Jason chuckled, although the sounds of his chuckle could barely be heard over the sound of Alex's tormented laughter as it erupted louder and louder from deep within him. "But we're just getting started here so I really can't answer that question for you…"

"*HAR, HAR, HAR, HAR, HAR, HAR, HAR, HAR, EEEEEEEEE!*" Alex laughed and screamed as Jason held his feet by the ankles real tight and methodically spun the vibrating bristles of the electric toothbrush over and over the bottoms of them.

Jason inhaled deeply as Alex's feet sweated like crazy…

"Jeez man, your feet are smelling worse and worse buddy boy," Jason said meanly to his captured nemesis. "I get the feeling that a good foot cleansing is in order for you here…"

"F–fuck that man, *ha, ha, ha, ha, ha, ha, ha, ha, ha, ha, ha, ha, ha!*" Alex cackled. "Just let me go! Fucking untie me and I'll be out of here faster than you can put your goddamned socks on!"

"Sorry to say bud, but I already got my socks on," Jason laughed and pressed the vibrating bristles of the toothbrush harder against the bottom of Alex's feet as he tickled them.

Alex managed to crane his neck a bit and looked at the suit, tie and dress shirt hanging in Jason's locker…

"D–don't you have to be somewhere soon? *HAHAHAHAHAHA!*" Alex asked through his uncontrolled bouts of laughter.

"I sure do, but right now I have more pressing and very ticklish issues here Alex me good buddy," Jason quipped and then ran the bristles of the electric toothbrush between Alex's toes, starting at his big toe on his right foot and moving down the line.

"*HOOO!*" Alex screamed in a high pitched tone of voice. "*OOOH no, not that, Jason*, not between my toes, *oh please, man!*"

Jason tickled in between Alex's toes for a good while, Alex laughed and hee hawed like a madman, and then to Alex's relief his opponent turned off the electric toothbrush. While Alex lay with his stomach against the bench and tried to catch his breath Jason tossed his electric toothbrush back into what he called his box of tricks. He set Alex's bare feet back on the floor and stood up to stretch his legs a bit.

"Hope you enjoyed that my good buddy," Jason said and reached down to give Alex's bubble butt a hard open handed swat.

"*Ouch! Fucker man!*" Alex rattled, his tied hands pressed against the floor. "That was a mean trick you played on me Jason!

But fuck it, you won this round! Untie me now and I'll be on my way… and…"

But as Alex spoke he looked up and saw that Jason was not to be seen…

"J–Jason? Jason, where the fuck are you man?" Alex called out, his deep voice bouncing off the walls of the locker room. "Fucking fucks man, don't leave me here like this Jason!"

Alex heaved himself upwards as much as possible, him not knowing how he was putting his ass on total display for me. The sight of his balls dangling down under his ass crack was a photo opportunity that any photographer who stalked celebrities would love to catch of the famous baseball player. Alex swore like a sailor and clenched his teeth as he tried in vain to get his hands untied.

"*Fuck*, fuck, *Jason*! Where the hell are you man?" Alex called out loudly. "You had your fun, okay? But you forgot to untie me…"

"I didn't forget shit Alex," Jason said as he sauntered back over to his tied up opponent, holding a plastic bottle of liquid soap in his hand. "I just needed to go to the bathroom to get something that I don't happen to have in my box of tricks…"

Jason chuckled meanly, sat back down on the bench with his back to Alex and placed the plastic bottle of liquid soap in front of him. Alex squawked angrily as Jason reached down, grabbed Alex's feet by his ankles and again secured them in front of himself by imprisoning them between his strong tree-trunk like thighs.

"Fuck man, what now?" Alex seethed as his stomach again rested on the bench, his tied up hands opening and closing in and out of fists under the bench. "You seem to have some kind of twisted obsession with my damned feet!"

"Now you get your feet cleaned up buddy boy," Jason said as he picked up the bottle of liquid soap. "Like I said man, your feet stink as much as you do out on the field…"

"*Fuck you*, man," Alex replied and then felt the sensation of the liquid soap being dripped onto the bottoms of his bare feet. "*Hey*, what the hell are you doing Jason?"

"Like I said man, I'm cleaning up your feet for you…" Jason laughed as he dripped a liberal amount of the liquid soap onto Alex's feet.

I saw Alex's toes curling back a bit as his feet were slathered with the soap…

"Fuck man, I don't need my goddamned feet cleaned, at least not by the likes of you…" Alex began, but then he was off again on a laughing tirade as Jason picked up a round bristled brush from his box of tricks and began gliding it over the bottoms, the arches, the soles, the heels and balls of Alex's soaped up feet. "*H–HEY HA, HA, HA, HA, HA, HA, HA, HA! OHHHRRR shhhiiittt man*, not again! *HAR, HAR, HAR, HAR, HAR, HAR, HAR!*"

Alex balled his tied up hands into a big fist and pressed them against the floor as tears of laughter formed in his eyes…

"A good feet cleaning indeed for my good buddy…" Jason quipped as he brushed Alex's soapy feet.

Jason's hand alternated back and forth and back and forth over Alex's feet with the brush, moving as fast as he could to make sure his opponent was thoroughly tickled.

"*OHHH gawd*, st–stop tickling me Jason! *HAHAHA HAHAHA HAHAHAHAHHAHA!*" Alex screeched. "Please man, stop fucking tickling me! *OHHHAHAHAHAHHHAHAHA!*"

"Who the fuck is tickling you me buddy?" Jason chortled sadistically. "I'm simply cleaning your feet for you man. I'm doing you a service here that no one in their right mind would want to do…"

That said Jason sniffed Alex's bare feet, made a sound of mocking disgust and worked harder at scrubbing them with his round brush. When he glided the brush over Alex's feet in a circular motion Alex laughed so hard that I thought he would pass out, but he was strong I'll give the baseball stud that much… he was strong. Actually, he needed to be very strong for what Jason had planned for him next…

After he had brush-scrubbed Alex's soapy feet for a good while it was now time to rinse the pretty baseball player off. Jason put down his round bristled brush, held Alex's soaped up feet tight in one hand and picked up a spray bottle of water. He sprayed Alex's feet as liberally with the water as he had done in slathering them with the liquid soap.

"Wh-what the fucking fuck now?" Alex quipped angrily and without realizing he did it he raised his sexy ass higher off the bench, placing himself in a real lusty looking position.

I could not help but notice how the crack of Alex's ass seemed to pout open and closed as he lay there in his helplessness…

"Now it's time to rinse your sweet feet buddy boy," Jason laughed and picked up a long stick Q-Tip, which had mounds of cotton on the end of it.

He began running the Q-Tip over and over the bottoms of Alex's wet soaped up feet…

"AAAAAAHHHAHAHHHAHAHA!" Alex again cried out as he was off again on a laughing tirade. "OOOHHH SSSSSHHHIIITTT MAN!"

The soapy water dripped off Alex's big feet as Jason ran that Q-Tip all over them in a circular motion and in between his toes.

"AHA, AHA, AHA, AHA, AHA, AHA, AHA, AHA, AHA, AHA, AHA, AHA!" Alex heaved, stuttering his laughter at that point. "J-Jason, please stop man, PLEASE STOP!"

"But Alex, if I don't dry your feet for you, you run the risk of contracting Athletes Foot," Jason said, sounding jovially sadistic.

"You really should be thanking me here. I mean, I would bet that not even your wife would wash your stinky feet for you…"

That said, Jason grinned meanly, held Alex's feet tighter and glided the Q-Tip faster and faster all over them…

Next, Alex found himself even more restrained as Jason squatted next to his captured opponent on the bench and proceeded to tie Alex's bare feet together under the bench. Alex squawked and swore, demanded to be released and seethed angrily as his so called buddy tied up his feet. What Jason did next I could not believe.

Standing there in just his navy blue dress socks and white briefs Jason looped a good length of rope around Alex's stomach region and tossed the slack of it up and over a beam in the ceiling above the lockers.

"OH GAWD Jason, what are you doing to me now?" Alex panted, his lips close enough to kiss Jason's dress socked foot as he the guy propped it up on the bench right in front of Alex's face.

The huge muscles in Jason's arms flexed involuntarily as he gave the rope looped around Alex's stomach region a good hard pull, yanking poor Alex up off the bench in an almost upside down U shape.

"H-HEY!" Alex croaked and then Jason tied off the ends of the rope, keeping Alex in a real humiliating position with that sexy, sexy ass of his raised up and the crack of it slightly parted, just as Jason wanted it.

"Oh me good buddy, you are in for it now," Jason laughed, gave Alex's ass a hard slap, reached into his box of tricks and produced a long stiff looking goose feather.

Alex craned his neck and saw what Jason had just taken from his box…

"OH NO, NO MAN! You wouldn't, you fucking wouldn't!" Alex gasped as Jason straddled the bench Alex was tied to and aimed the tip of the feather directly at Alex's gaping hole.

"AAAAYYYYHAHAHAAA!" was once again the sound that filled the locker room as Alex went into a new laughing fit. "JASON, this is sick! HAHAHAHAHA! FUCKER man, don't be ticklin' my damned, HAHAhahahahah, my damned asshole!"

With a look of sadistic glee on his villainously handsome face Jason burrowed the goose feather into Alex's asshole, twirled it around in there and meanly tickled his baseball nemesis in what had to be the most mortifying of ways…

Alex farted a couple of times and Jason quipped, "Fuck man, you really do stink buddy boy…"

The sound of the two men laughing filled the locker room, one of the men laughing because he was in total control of the situation, the other man laughing because he had no control whatsoever of the situation…

After a while Jason extracted the feather from deep within Alex's asshole, trailed it over the back of Alex's well-muscled thighs, the backs of his knees and over the bottoms of his bare feet. All the while Alex laughed and danced on the end of the rope that Jason had tethered him with. Then, Alex's loud and raucous squeals again filled the locker room as Jason swiveled the feather back into his asshole once more… .

"AAAAYYYYRRRHAHA FUCKING FUCKS!" Alex cawed. "HAHAHAHAHHA!"

"HUUUHHH! Wh-what the fucking fucks are you up to now Jason?" Alex seethed a short while later.

The captive baseball player now found himself off the bench and (temporarily) untied. Sadly for Alex he was now blindfolded, one of his own smelly navy blue sweat socks tied over his eyes and pulled down just over his nose, so that each time the guy inhaled he was treated to a nose-full of his own sweaty foot raunchiness.

"AW man, blindfold a guy with one of his own stinky sweat socks?" Alex railed. "You can't get lower than that you bastard!" Jason again had Alex by his upper arms, holding his opponent in a real tight grip as Alex struggled futilely in darkness.

"Let go of me man, come on," Alex squawked, his legs kicking out in front of him as he struggled uselessly.

"Man, you really are a struggler," Jason laughed and heaved Alex forward so that his forehead again connected with his locker.

The sound of Alex's head hitting the locker was a loud clang...

"AAWWWHHH man, fucking dirty fighter..." Alex cooed softly as he slid downward to his knees in front of the locker he had just been rammed against yet again.

He gripped the sides of the locker as his head had to be spinning in a reverse orbit. For some reason the knot in the back of Alex's head in his sock/blindfold was erotic looking somehow. As he gasped for breath, sitting on his knees and gripping the sides of the locker Jason reached down, grabbed Alex by one of his biceps and hauled the poor guy to his feet...

"Coming up, part two of your tickle torments buddy boy," Jason laughed as Alex stood next to him blindfolded with his teeth clenched real tight.

Alex balled his hand into a fist but Jason was too fast for him. He swung his blindfolded opponent quickly around by his arm, again slamming him into the locker, this time bodily...

"AAAWWW..." Alex moaned as he again hit the floor.

This time, when poor Alex came back around he found himself in yet another humiliating and tied up position on the bench in front of Jason's locker...

"OOHHH… dirty fighter… dirty fucking fighter," Alex moaned as he opened his eyes, relieved that he was no longer blindfolded, but irate at the fact that he found to his dismay that he was again tied up on the bench. "GODDAMNIT JASON, god damn you, untie me you fucker!"

"Now, now Alex me buddy, you know that that's not going to happen for a while yet…" Jason laughed meanly.

Alex took in the fact that this time he was lying on the bench on his back, his muscular chest pointing up at the ceiling along with his jutted up nipples and his hard throbbing cock. Alex's hands were tied at the wrists underneath him with his arms dangling at the sides of the bench he was on. To his utter dismay he saw that his bare feet were propped up atop a filled gym bag that was tied to the end of the bench. Alex's elevated feet were tied to the gym bag.

"Wh-what is this man?" Alex croaked angrily, struggling in the tight bondage, swinging his musculature back and forth on the bench, causing his erect cock to swing against his stomach area, his big sweaty balls resting atop his thighs.

"As I said buddy boy, this is part two of your tickle torments…" Jason laughed and delighted in the sight of Alex trying desperately to get his feet freed, obviously knowing what he in for now. "And this time we're going to mix tickling with a game of "Guess what I've written on the bottom of your foot."

Jason sat down at the end of the bench and held up a ball point pen…

Alex's eyes opened wide in sheer terror…

"HOLY FUCKING FUCKS and shit man, what, what the hell are you doing Jason?" Alex quipped, no longer smiling.

"Here's how the game works Alex me buddy," Jason said with a maniacal looking grin on his face. "I'm going to write names of your teammates on the bottom of your feet, or I might write baseball terms. You need to concentrate on the motion of my pen and guess correctly what I'm writing. If you guess correctly I'll let you out of here. If you guess incorrectly we move on to the next thing I write on your feet. It's that simple buddy boy."

"B-but, but Jason, you don't know what the fucking fuck that will do to me man!" Jason pleaded and his hard cock dribbled more pre cum.

"Oh but Alex, I do know what it will do to you, I do know, it will tickle you, it will tickle your feet," Jason said and pressed the tip of the pen against the sole of Alex's right naked foot.

"OH GAWD MAN!" Alex screeched.

"Concentrate now buddy," Jason said meanly. "Concentrate, you're getting out of here depends on it!"

"B-but I won't be able to concentrate when you're t-tickling me man..." Alex begged. "JASON, please don't... please..."

With that maniacal looking grin on his face Jason started scrawling the pen across the sole of Alex's right foot.

"D, that was a D, ha, ha, ha, ha, ha, ha, ha, ha, ha, ha, ha, ha!" Alex crowed.

"Pretty good so far buddy boy," Jason laughed, held Alex's foot by the toes and scrawled the next letter.

"FUCK, I thought for sure that would have been an E on the next one, ha, ha, ha, ha, ha, ha, ha, ha, ha!"

"Lost your concentration already buddy boy?" Jason asked snippily.

"Th-thought you were goin' to write Derek," Alex cawed through his laughter as Jason scrawled more on his poor foot.

"Ah, thinkin' about your best team buddy huh?" Jason laughed as he wrote and wrote. "I wonder what he would think if he could see you now. But no way will I make it that easy for you buddy boy..."

"Th-that just felt like a letter L I think," Alex called out. "HARHARHARHAR! FUCK, what is that you're writing?"

"Now if I tell you the game won't be any fun would it?" Jason asked Alex, chuckling as he said it.

When Jason finished the first word, which Alex had not figured out was "double play" he began a new word, telling his opponent to try again, to really concentrate this time.

"PPPFFFHHHAHAHAHA! O-Okay, that felt like a letter J, or maybe an H, oh fuck me! HAHAHAHAHAHHAHAHAHA!" Alex cackled like a hyena.

"Wrong on both guesses," Jason said and began writing a third word.

"HAHAHAHAHA! JASON, please stop this man!" Alex cried out crazily as Jason wrote some more on his poor trapped feet.

"Stop what man?" Jason quipped as he wrote. "I told you, this is just a game buddy boy."

"J-Jason, I'll get ink poisoning!" Alex cackled. "HARHARHARHAR!"

"Relax buddy boy, I'm not pressing that hard," Jason said in his defense and scrawled more letters on the bottoms of Alex's feet. "Okay man, the next word I'm going to begin on your right foot and finish it on your left foot. You ready buddy? Concentrate now, concentrate…"

"Ea-easy for you to say man, you're the not the poor sap of a guy all tied up and laughing his damned head off…" Alex replied angrily. "HAHAHAHAHAHA!"

"Well, that all just makes the game all the more challenging for you, right?" Jason asked meanly.

"O-Okay, that was a letter S I think," Alex laughed and Jason simply nodded his head "no." "OH FUCK ME MAN, what a fucked up situation this is!"

By the time Jason stopped writing on Alex's feet both of the tied up baseball players bare feet were completely covered in ink scrawls. Even Alex's toes had letters written on them. When Jason had written on Alex's toes the poor guy could have flown off the bench, if he wasn't tied down to it that is...

"HAHAHAHAHAHAAA!" Alex laughed as Jason put his pen away in his box of tricks. "FUCKING fucks, I didn't get any right did I?"

"That's why you're still here me good buddy..." Jason said. "But now my time is running short Alex my ticklish friend. I can stay to help you get that ink off your feet and then I'm outa here..."

"FUCK THAT MAN, I'll wash the ink off myself," Alex said angrily as Jason untied his ink messed feet. "You've done enough to me already you asshole! I don't need you showering me again..."

Jason stuck the rope that had been tied around Alex's feet into the waistband of his underpants; no doubt he planned to tie his buddy yet again...

"Who said anything about showering you buddy?" Jason asked Alex as he reached down to untie his opponent's hands. "I'm gonna clean up your inky feet in the foot scrubber we have in this locker room."

"F-FOOT SCRUBBER?" Alex asked as he was hauled up off the bench by his wrists, Jason holding him real tight. "What foot scrubber? I never heard of such a thing!"

"Well, that's 'cause your team doesn't get the luxuries we get here in our locker room buddy boy," Jason said, clenched his teeth and gripped Alex's wrists tighter.

"Foot scrubber, this should be interesting to see..." Alex seethed and struggled in Jason's strong grasp.

"Now, if you don't want to go swinging head-first against my locker again you'll be real cooperative Alex me buddy of buds..." Jason said merrily.

Holding Alex's wrists in a tight grip Jason half dragged half walked him toward the rear of the locker room. It looked like the two men were involved in some kind of erotic dance as Jason plodded Alex along by holding his wrists tight. Jason in his long dress socks and white briefs and Alex totally naked with his erection swinging back and forth and his balls dangling real low made for a real kinky sight let me tell you.

"Fucker, let go of me man," Alex ranted in Jason's face. "I DO NOT NEED MY DAMNED FEET SCRUBBED! I'll get this goddamned ink off myself!"

When Alex saw the device that Jason planned to use on him to supposedly clean his ink scrawled feet was when he again began struggling.

"FUCK, fuck, that's no foot scrubber, that's a goddamned shoe shining machine!" Alex grunted angrily. "Th-that's for us guys to use when we get out of our baseball uniforms and put on our street clothes!"

"You really are one smart guy, even though you stink Alex," Jason laughed and hauled Alex off his feet by his wrists, the huge muscles in his biceps straining with his heavy load.

To Alex's dismay he again found himself propelled against a locker, his muscular back and the back of his head taking the brunt of the blows this time.

"UUHHNNFFF!" Alex groaned and placed his hands atop his head as he slid to the floor in front of the locker.

As Alex sat there with his head spinning he watched through hazy vision as Jason set up a straight backed chair behind the shoe shining device and then squatted down to open the two panels in the device where a man would stick his shoed feet in. In this case it was Alex's bare feet that would be housed in the device. Jason looked down at the various round bristled brushes in the machine and then looked over at his stunned baseball opponent.

"Okay me good buddy, your throne awaits you," Jason said in a fiendish sounding tone of voice.

Jason stepped over to Alex, reached down and hauled him again off his feet by his wrists and swinging the guy upwards till he was perched on one of his muscular shoulders... Alex's head spun and he came around gradually as Jason was lowering his bare feet toward the two open panels in the shoe shine device...

"FUCKER MAN, NO NO! Don't lock my goddamned feet in that thing you sick fuck!" Alex pleaded as Jason dangled the poor guy's bare feet over the electric shoe shining machine. "Jason, put me down man! Oh God of gods put me down you fucker! This machine is to shine shoes, not bare feet!"

The round brushes with the whirl-around bristles within the device mocked Alex, calling to him, beckoning in a hungry fashion it would seem...

"OH FUCK NO, NO JASON!" Alex begged as Jason lowered Alex into the shoe shining device.

Alex felt as if the bristles in the machine were literally swallowing his feet as he was plunged in. Once his feet were encased within all the bristles Jason pushed Alex down into the chair set up behind the shoe shine machine and slammed the doors of it shut.

Before Alex could react after being thrust into the chair Jason was quickly roping him tightly to it, using the lengths of rope he had stowed in his underpants waistband...

"BASTARD, bastard, what a shitty way to treat a poor guy," Alex moaned and groaned, jostling his feet and trying to get them out of the locked shoe shine device.

Once Alex was securely tied to the chair Jason squatted in front of his trapped feet and placed his fingertip on the on/off switch on the machine.

"And off you go again to tickle land buddy boy..." Jason said, almost singing and switched the machine on.

"HARHARHARHARHAR! OH GOOD GAWD, it, it's tickling my damned feet!" Alex crowed as the bristles within the shoeshine device spun over and over and over his feet trapped inside it.

Alex writhed in the chair and his erection waved in the wind as he was unmercifully tickled yet again...

"You know man, with that boner you got I would think you're really enjoying what I'm doing to you here today buddy boy," Jason laughed and cupped Alex's chin in his hand for a moment as he laughed and laughed.

"Th-that's a crock of shit, buddy boy," Alex snarled. "HAHAHAHAHAHHAHAAHA, my big sausage sized cock just has a mind all its own! HARHARHARHAR!"

"Well, while you're enjoying that I'm going to go and put on the rest of my suit," Jason said and walked away from Alex as he laughed and laughed...

"NO, NO, JASON, don't leave me here man! HAHAHAHAHAHA! Please man, untie me first!" Alex begged, watching as Jason's hot briefs covered backside sauntered away from him.

I watched from my hiding place as my hero Jason got himself all prettied up in his suit and tie, taking his sweet time at his locker as he dressed... I took his red "high" socks from my pocket and again held the toes section of them to my nose and mouth. It was a magical feeling, sniffing Jason's mangy scented socks and watching him as he dressed in a more formal kind of attire. I looked at Jason's thick red sweat socks in my hand and then at the handsome guy's big navy blue nylon socked feet as he slid them into a pair of well-shined black cap-toes. As Alex's helpless peals of laughter filled the locker room Jason stepped over to a full-length mirror and checked his appearance in his reflection... The look in his eyes was one of satisfaction mixed with a sinister kind of lust. He glanced in the direction of Alex's laughter and then looked down at his box of tricks...

Before putting his box of tricks back in his locker however he grinned one more time and took two tubes from the box...

Still grinning he walked back over to the laughing and cackling Alex...

"Well, I'm almost ready to get out of here buddy boy," Jason said. "How do I look?"

"HARHARHARHAR! YOU look real sweet, okay?" Alex replied, his laughter sounding uncontrolled and totally angry at that point. "BUT NO JASON, no, don't leave me here like this man!"

"Now would I do something like that to you my good buddy?" Jason laughed and squatted down at the shoe shining device.

He turned off the machine and Alex breathed a short-lived sigh of relief...

"TH-thank you man, thank you," Alex said breathlessly.

But then Alex watched as his opponent opened the panels on the shoe shining device that his feet were encased in and held up the first tube he had taken from his box of tricks... Alex saw that it was a tube of aloe cream.

"Wh-what are you doing Jason?" Alex squawked in what sounded like mortal terror as Jason poured a liberal amount of the cream onto the brushes surrounding Alex's feet in the shoe shining machine. "Jason, no, no!"

Alex tried to pry his feet upwards and out of the machine but Jason pressed down on his knees and pushed Alex's feet back in. Next, Jason held up a tube of liquid soap.

"Time to clean that ink off your feet buddy boy..." Jason laughed as he poured the liquid soap into the machine next.

"JASON, let me out of this man!" Alex said demandingly as his captor slammed the panels shut again on the machine, trapping his feet within it once more. "Jason, those brushes are all slippery now man! If you turn this goddamned machine on now I'll be tickled even worse…"

"Bingo buddy boy," Jason said and flicked the on/off switch.

As Jason stood up straight he grinned down at Alex as the poor guy once again went off on a laughing tirade…

"HARHARHARHAR!" Alex laughed as the now much lubricated brushes in the machine did their work.

I watched as Jason strode back to his locker to put the tubes of aloe cream and liquid soap away…

"DON-DON'T leave me here like this Jason, pleeeeeeaasseee man!" Alex cried out laughingly. "HARHARHARHAR!"

He tried in vain to get his feet out of the device but it looked to me as if his feet were being sucked further and further into it as the poor guy laughed and laughed and laughed…

As I watched from my hiding spot I suddenly felt a hand grip my shoulder from behind…

"Hey Rick," Jason said to me, sidling up in front of me and glancing at his red socks as they stuck out of my front pants pocket. "Still here I see…"

"Uh yes, Jason, I, uh, I was just… uh, finishing up…" I stammered as the handsome baseball player reached forward and extracted his socks from my pocket.

"A souvenir Rick?" he asked me, holding up the socks and I gasped in sheer terror. "I got to say, I'm honored man."

I breathed a sigh of relief as he handed me back the socks and glanced in the direction of the cackling and laughing Alex…

"You know I can't leave him here like that indefinitely," Jason said to me.

"No, of course not," I said nervously.

"So here's the deal Rick, you can keep my smelly socks, I'm sure someday they'll be worth something when I'm old and retired," Jason said, grinning at me. "What I want for you to do is let that machine scrub/tickle that pretty boy's feet for a good half hour and then you can have the honor of releasing him… or maybe not…"

At that we both chuckled meanly…

A short while later Jason had left the locker room…

I had some fiendish ideas of my own where the pretty boy baseball player Alex was concerned…

I dashed quickly and silently over to the spot where Jason had taken Alex's navy blue sweat socks off his feet before tickling them bare. I picked up one of the long sweat socks and made my way stealthily back over to the tied up and laughing Alex…

His laughter was enough to mask the sound of my approach from behind him… As I stepped up to him I stretched his long sweat sock out, and then, before he knew what was happening draped it over his eyes from behind…

"HAHAHAHAHAHHAHAHA! H-HEY!" Alex laughed loudly. "WH-what the fucking fucks? WHO IS THAT?"

Smiling meanly now myself I squatted down in front of the tied up tickled baseball player and grabbed his erection in my fist, squeezing it tight…

"UUULLLPPP, HAHAHAHAHAHAHA! HEY, who are you man? FUCKER, you got me by the cock!" Alex crowed, his head thrown back as he laughed in darkness now.

I began stroking his cock and said, "You know Mr. Alex, after a man shoots his load he's even more tickle sensitive…"

"HOOO NO NO NO!" Alex pleaded. "OHHH FUCKING FUCKS!"

A few more good strokes and Alex shot a load big enough to choke a horse…

His laughter increased about one hundred and fifty percent…

ABOUT THE AUTHOR

Christopher Trevor

Christopher Trevor was born in July 1963 and grew up in New York City. As soon as he was old enough to know how he began writing fiction and has been writing gay erotic/fetish stories for the past ten to twelve years at this point. He became an avid reader as well from the time he knew how and reads everything from fiction, to non-fiction to biographies of interesting and unusual people, people

who have made a difference or who have paved the way for others. Christopher attributes his writing artistic inspiration to artists such as Etienne, Tom of Finland, Tagame, The Hun, and most notably Joe T, who Christopher has had the pleasure of speaking with and even meeting over the last few years. Christopher states, "Joe T encouraged me to write about my fetish because I was embarrassed about it at the time. Joe T said that when we are embarrassed about something that makes it even more enticing somehow." Christopher totally agreed and never stopped writing in this genre. Erotic writers who inspired Christopher Trevor were: Tom Shaw (author of "That Day at the Quarry), C.S. White (author of Big Sur), Larry Townsend (author of countless erotic novels), and Mason Powell (author of the classic story "The Brig.")

Christopher discovered that not only did he enjoy writing erotic tales but that after his first bondage experience he had a genuine flair for it. Writing to erotic oriented magazines about his first bondage experience truly opened the floodgates for Christopher where this style of writing is concerned. Christopher thanks the handsome and muscular "Greg" for that experience way back in time. Christopher took "Creative Writing" courses every semester during his high school years and while other friends of his stopped writing what they loved to write about as time went on Christopher never let a day go by when he didn't write something... "I feel that if I don't write every day I will die," Christopher has said many times over.

Foot fetish stories and all things related; spanking fetish, erotic shaving, muscle bondage, tickle torture, and hardcore stories are just a few of the areas of gay eroticism that Christopher enjoys writing about and inspiring in others as well. As one internet buddy said to Christopher where the black socks fetish is concerned, "Until I started talking with you I never gave a thought to my socks when I got dressed for work in the morning. Now when I pull my dress socks on every morning I get a chill up my spine."

Christopher is proud of the erotic effect he has on people...

Christopher Trevor is also the author of:

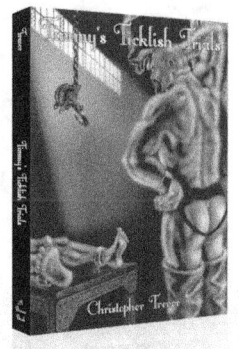

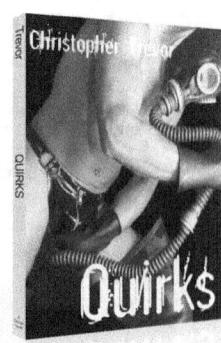

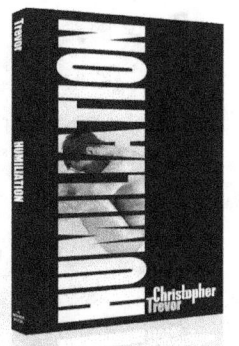

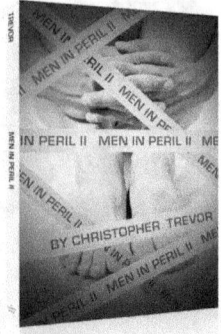

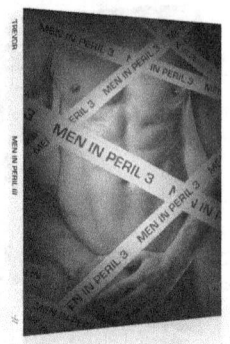

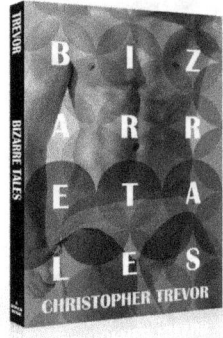

www.ingramcontent.com/pod-product-compliance
Lightning Source LLC
Chambersburg PA
CBHW051150260626
47170CB00005B/2043